Western Literature Series

Richard Yañez

El Paso del Norte

››› *Stories on the Border* ‹‹‹

University of Nevada Press ▲▲ Reno & Las Vegas

Western Literature Series
University of Nevada Press, Reno,
Nevada 89557 USA
www.unpress.nevada.edu

Copyright © 2003 by Richard Yañez
Manufactured in the United States
of America
Design by Carrie House
Library of Congress Cataloging-in-
Publication Data
Yañez, Richard, 1967–
El Paso del Norte : stories on the
border / Richard Yañez
p. cm. — (Western literature series)
ISBN 978-0-87417-533-2 (pbk. : alk. paper)
ISBN 978-0-87417-904-0 (ebook)
1. Mexican-American Border
Region—Fiction. 2. Mexican
Americans—Fiction. I. Title
II. Series
PS3625.A677 E4 2003
813'.6—dc21   2002011993

The paper used in this book meets
the requirements of American
National Standard for Information
Sciences—Permanence of Paper
for Printed Library Materials,
ANSI/NISO Z39.48-1992 (R2002).
Binding materials were selected
for strength and durability.

This book has been reproduced as a digital reprint.

For my dad and mom and only brother
Para Polo y Chuy

Seen and Unseen

The Río Grande is crooked here where it has claimed land and returned it and reclaimed it many times.

KEVIN MCILVOY, *Hyssop*

>>> **Contents** <<<

>>> *Acknowledgments* <<<

The author gratefully acknowledges the original publishers of the following stories:

"Desert View" in *third coast* (2001); excerpt from "Amoroza Tires" and "Good Time" in *flyway* (2000); "Río Bravo" in *Saguaro* (1996); "Lucero's Mkt." in *Revista Bilingüe/Bilingual Review* (1998); excerpt from "Sacred Heart," number 15 in the Chicano Chapbook Series, edited by Gary Soto (1997); "I&M Plumbing" in *Mirrors Beneath the Earth: Short Fiction by Chicano Writers*, edited by Ray Gonzalez (Curbstone Press, 1992) and in *Our Working Lives: Short Stories of People and Work*, edited by Bonnie Jo Campbell and Larry Smith (Bottom Dog Press, 2000).

The author also thanks the following for their guidance, friendship, and cariño: Rick DeMarinis, Irma Carrillo, Ricardo Sánchez, Dagoberto Gilb, Rose Avalos, Kevin McIlvoy, Rob Wilder, Robert Boswell, Denise Chávez, Antonya Nelson, Rick Lucas, Andrea Foege, Todd McKinney, Ricardo Aguilar Melantzón, Alberto Ríos, Karla Elling, Ron Carlson, Demetria Martínez, Rigoberto González, Stuart Dybek, Mike McNally, Michael Guerra, Thea Kuticka, Ryan McKee, and Sandy Crooms.

>>> *El Paso del Norte* <<<

>>> *Desert Vista* <<<

The mud balls appeared the day I kissed Ana Garza.

Wet dirt from the nearby canal clung like brown hands to the front windows, garage doors, tile roof. Our house—covered in Frisbee-sized chocolate chips—looked good enough to eat.

I didn't mind that I had to wash and scrub instead of being free to shoot baskets when I came home after school. And when I drank from the mouth of the hose, I thought of how Ana Garza's lips had been pressed on mine. My tongue had touched hers.

It might've been the inside of her bottom lip. But who cared? We'd kissed.

That evening, while my dad interrogated me and my older brother, I suckled a mango. This was after I'd tried a peach and a nectarine. When my mom said, "I thought you didn't like fruit," I shook my head and continued to kiss the orange flesh hidden inside the spotted, yellow-green skin.

I wanted to ask my brother, who I knew had kissed more than one girl, if I had done it right. When I nudged him, sitting next to me on the den sofa, I saw that all he and my dad were interested in was who might've used our house for target practice. I flicked dried mud off my corduroys and wondered if we had any more mangoes. My dad marched off and left me and my brother in front of a rerun on TV.

"Maybe it's those guys you flipped off," I said, pretending to care about the other big news earlier today. "Remember when they were scoping out your car?"

"Naw, those guys were older. These are kids."

"Kids?" I said, licking the sweet off my lips. "What makes you think there was more than one?"

"Man, did you see all those mud balls? There were about a hundred."

"Thirty-three," I said and nodded.

Judging from my brother's tone, he appeared to have taken this very personal. And since he and I rarely talked anymore, I made the most out of this opportunity.

"Maybe it's *cholos*," I said.

"Cholos?" he asked curiously. "What do you know about cholos?"

"I know cholos." I liked the way "cholos" sounded and how it opened my mouth, like if I was blowing a bubble.

An image of a cholo strutted into my mind: a brown-skinned boy wearing a hairnet and a starched T-shirt and khakis, with a neatly folded bandanna drooping out of his back pocket.

"How do you know?" My brother swatted the top of my head, something our dad used to do when we were little.

"There's this guy in my English class. Antonio. Tony. Tony Ayala. He flipped the teacher off one time."

"And that makes him a cholo?"

"Doesn't it? And he writes it too."

"Writes what?"

"Those cool letters. The thin, curvy ones." I moved my index finger in the space between us. "Like on the Declaration of Independence."

My brother was cracking up, so I kept going.

"When I gave Tony Ayala some paper, he wrote out my name, El Ruly, and called me an 'es-say.'"

"You mean 'ése,'" he said and again swatted my head. "Don't you know Spanish?"

"I didn't know that's what cholos talked," I said.

Before falling asleep, I thought about how clean our house was when we first moved here from La Loma less than a year ago. A yard full of grass. Tall mulberries. And like every house in Desert Vista—"Best View in East El Paso," as advertised on billboards—our four-bedroom house was beige stucco. Our front doors were the only things different from any of the other homes. My dad bought ours across the Border. After sanding the pine, he painted them Oaxaca Blue.

With my family's move, I also transferred to my first public school, Desert Vista Junior High. When my brother said he was glad that he wouldn't have to wear a uniform, I lied and said I'd also hated the blue-and-gray-plaid shirts and shiny loafers we wore at Father Yermo.

From the stories I'd heard from my cousins, who all went to public school, I had many expectations. Bigger hallways, my own locker, sports teams, a cafeteria with better snack machines. None of these was the first thing I noticed at Desert Vista Junior High. As soon as I arrived at the school, I saw "the writing on the wall," an expression I heard on TV.

It was hard not to notice the graffiti scrawled all over the buildings. The letters were curved and bent like the ironwork of houses in Juárez. I wondered if the words and phrases were there to make my transition easier. Since I only really used Spanish the few times we visited my grandparents in La Loma, much of the graffiti was foreign to me. And given that I couldn't make out all the ornate letters, it might as well have been in another language altogether. I know I certainly felt that way when a note appeared in my locker.

VATO WATCH YOUR SORRY ASS
WE DONT KNOW WERE YOU FROM
PUTO YOUR NOT FROM HERE
PONTE TRUCHA WERE CHECKING
YOU OUT DONT THINK WE CANT
MESS YOU UP ESE
El Sapo   V L K
c / s

And like that, the words I tried to ignore in the hallways, all over desks, and on bathroom stalls had found their way into my hands.

That day, which was during my first month at Desert Vista Junior High, I was only able to decipher the note's shorter words. After studying it alone in my bedroom, afraid to show it to anyone, I put most of it together. When I found out that "VLK" stood for "Varrio Los Kennedys," one of the baddest gangs around, I wished I hadn't worked so hard to read the note.

For weeks I walked around scared. I knew of gangs, but I didn't know anyone who'd been threatened by one, much less someone who was a part of one.

I carried and read the note all the time. During morning announcements. In the lunch line. At PE. I didn't know why. Maybe if I read it enough, I thought, it might lose its threat.

Every day that I came home from school not messed up, the note became less and less intimidating. I finally tucked the worn sheet of paper in the back of my sock drawer, where I also kept my communion rosary and a *TV Guide* cover of Wonder Woman. I decided it must've been someone playing a joke or some kind of initiation. Though every time I saw the letters VLK freshly spray-painted around school, I made sure to look over my shoulder. And I always knew El Sapo could be any one of the cholos who cruised the hallways before, during, and after class.

>>> As I walked to catch the bus the next morning, I paused at the end of our street. The mud balls had left me suspicious of where we lived. In the time since we'd moved to Desert Vista, a barrier of wooden posts and metal rails with a NO PASSING sign had been put up. County workers planted it right where the sidewalk ended, in front of an empty lot.

When I asked my parents why the neighborhood association wanted to split up Nottingham Drive, they said, "You'll be safer. We all will." I hadn't felt unsafe in Desert Vista, but I didn't say anything. I trusted my parents.

Santiago Reyes lived on the other side of the barrier. He was my new friend. After the cholo note, I'd made an effort to make friends. We took bus #12 to and from school, and when I saw him carrying a basketball, I started sitting next to him. I invited him over to my house to shoot baskets in the driveway.

I'd wanted to try out for the school's basketball team, "the Mighty Giants," when I transferred to Desert Vista Junior High, but I was afraid I wasn't good enough.

Santiago said he would've tried out but that Coach Tapia didn't like him. When I asked why, he said he'd called Coach a *joto*. I laughed along with Santiago as he faked left and ducked in to make a layup. "Joto," I repeated. While I wasn't exactly sure what "joto" meant in English, I also enjoyed the way "joto" blew out of my mouth. It rhymed with "cholo."

"Why does your mom keep looking out the window?" Santiago asked after I fouled him on a jump shot. "She think you run away?"

"Naw, she's watching for cholos."

"Cholos?" Santiago asked, catching his breath. "What are you talking about?"

"Nothing, ignore her."

"C'mon, aren't we friends, ése?" His smile stretched into a wide u.

"Okay, but let me ask you something," I said.

"Go for it." He spun the ball on his index finger.

"Do you know any cholos?"

"My brothers were," he said while he aimed a free throw shot, "but now they're roofers. Like our father." *Swish.*

I ended up telling Santiago how, in addition to mud-balling our house, someone had toilet-papered the houses closest to the barrier. The neighborhood association had another meeting. When my dad came home, he said, "That's it." I wanted to ask what "it" was but I didn't.

I told Santiago that I thought it was probably some older kids horsing around. Of his six brothers, two attended Ysleta High along with my brother.

As my best friend and I played game after game of HORSE— him beating me more times by making a basket for each letter— we both agreed that high school was probably way more fun than stupid junior high.

Tired and thirsty, I invited Santiago inside for a snack. At the kitchen table, I savored a mango while he finished a peanut butter sandwich in three bites. When he caught me kissing the mango, I got nervous.

"You want some?" I asked, hoping he didn't.

"Naw, they make my mouth itch."

We were about to go mess with my brother's stuff when my mom entered the kitchen. I was too busy eating my mango and forgot to introduce Santiago. My mom looked him over.

"He's my friend," I said, wiping my chin with the back of my hand. "We ride the bus together."

My mom kept staring as if she knew him from somewhere other than through the window.

"Do you live in that big house with the birdbath out front?" Santiago shook his head. "We don't have but one bath. And my brothers leave it full of hairs."

My mom laughed. I laughed. Santiago smiled.

"I'm going to start supper, so," my mom said and motioned for us to leave the kitchen, her favorite part of the new house, I'd heard her tell my dad.

Santiago said he'd better go and do some homework. We both hated homework, so I knew he was lying. I worried that my mom might've said something wrong.

When I walked him down Nottingham Drive, I decided he would be the first one I told about Ana Garza. Feathered, pecan-pie-brown hair. Eyes like my favorite shooties. No pimples. How we'd kissed at her locker and before PE. The second time, I put my hands on her waist. "Her hips?" Santiago asked. "Yeah, her hips," I corrected myself. We both agreed that I was lucky to be kissing.

I instinctively stopped before we got to the barrier.

Although I'd ridden my bike up and down Nottingham Drive when we first moved here, I now saw it differently. As two sides. And I wondered if Santiago was also aware of this other side.

We shook hands in the long way that only best friends had. And then I watched him climb over the barrier like Spider-Man before I turned and ran home.

››› News of me and Ana Garza kissing bounced through Desert Vista Junior High faster than the story of my house being mud-balled. Many of the guys gave me a hard time—asking if we'd *Frenched,* when was she gonna give me a *hickey,* and if I'd touched her *chi chis.* Like graffiti and cholos, I learned, kissing had its own vocabulary.

At lunch while I scrambled for the ball on the blacktop, I made sure that Ana Garza was watching. She whistled each time I made a basket. I wanted to get called out, so I could go over and kiss her. But the truth was that I wasn't brave enough to do that in front of the whole school.

One of Ana Garza's friends, Gracie Levario, came over when I went for a drink of water. I would've thought Gracie was pretty if I wasn't kissing Ana Garza. Gracie handed me a note. When I saw Ana Garza's handwriting—thick and slanted—I couldn't wait to read it. I didn't get a chance because the bell rang. I stopped by my locker and hurried to English.

As Mrs. Harris went over some homework assignment, I thought of how public school was better than Catholic school. It wasn't all about long assemblies, parent-teacher conferences, and weekly confessions. Kissing had changed all that. Ana Garza and I went from planning to bump into each other between fourth and fifth periods to holding hands as we waited in the lunch line. And now she had written me a note saying that she wanted me to go to Western Playland Amusement Park. She and her friends were going, and I had to go. Yes, I had to. No matter what.

When I saw Mrs. Harris walking my way, I tucked the note in my corduroys and opened my journal. I counted the check marks on the inside cover. Kissing for the ninth time was as good, if not better, as the first time. That was for sure. If it had been up to me, I would've written about the sweetness of kissing, not "How I See Myself in Ten Years." I'd been writing in my journal almost every day, and English was becoming my favorite subject.

Ever since my bike was stolen, I'd been taking bus #12 home from school. I had no clue who took my bike from our front yard. I suspected El Sapo—whichever cholo he was—since it disappeared around the time I got the threatening note. I'd written in my journal how he might've converted my BMX to one of those lowrider bikes I'd seen at Ascarate Park. All chrome and mirrors. Candy-apple red. *Low and slow.*

It didn't matter, anyway. I liked the bus. Boys and girls' voices in Spanish and English—and a mouthwatering combination of the two, like a gordita and burrito plate—echoed inside the cavernous metal body. On the bus ride to and from school, I'd gaze out the windows as we drove along North Loop Road. The rows of cotton fields reminded me of my brown corduroys, and the chile fields blurred by me like the green lines on notebook paper. I'd gotten A's and B's on my essays but D's in penmanship. "You think faster than you can write," Mrs. Harris wrote on my paper. "Stay within the lines."

On the bus, I told Santiago about going to Western Playland. I was surprised that he was interested. I thought he'd say that riding the El Bandido Roller Coaster and the Matador Twister was dumb. I guessed why he wanted to go. Before we split up at the barrier, he made sure to ask about Ana Garza and her friend Letty Sida. "Yeah, for sure they're going," I said. When Santiago smiled, his mouth stayed slightly open as if in anticipation. Pretty soon, we both might be kissing.

>>> One day after school, when Santiago had to help his father shingle a roof, I came home to find another boy in our driveway. I was more surprised to see my mom home so early than to see her clutching a broom next to the boy holding our water hose.

"What are—" I started to say.

"Get inside," my mom said, her eyes fixed on the boy. "I'll be in soon."

For a second I thought she was addressing the boy. When she repeated herself—"Get inside now, Raul Luis."—I registered her tone, not to mention her use of my two first names, and I rushed inside.

From my brother's bedroom window, I peeked outside. After the boy sprayed water where my mom pointed, he dried each window with one of my dad's old T-shirts. He had to jump to reach the higher windows.

While I didn't recognize the boy, I didn't think of him as a stranger. Face, hair, eyes—all brown—like most at Desert Vista Junior High.

I wanted to question him. Do you have a hairnet? How about a bandanna? I decided he wasn't a cholo when I noticed his pants weren't creased, no sharp lines running down his legs like fences.

When I saw him run toward the barrier, I figured that's what side he lived on. I couldn't spend any more time thinking about it. My mom came in the house. I raced to my room and took out my language arts book. The "C-" on my last report card was enough for my mom to say that she and my dad had "their eye on me." Although I'd also heard this expression followed by laughter on TV, it still made me nervous.

I didn't tell my parents why homework no longer mattered. Math, science, history, all boring compared to Ana Garza, cholos, bus rides. I hoped that they wouldn't make me confess any of it.

At dinner that night, we made it through half of a meat loaf, most of the instant mashed potatoes, and two cans of cream corn before my mom said anything.

"Don't you think you should tell your father?" She sat in the chair across from me.

I raised my eyes from my plate and swallowed. "Huh?" A chunk of meat loaf didn't slide down as easily as the potatoes.

"You know what I mean." She kept her eye on me while my dad and brother kept theirs on their plates.

I shook my head and reached for my bottle of Mr. PiBB.

"Maybe this will help you remember." She pulled something from her lap and tossed it on the table like Mrs. Seymour returning the science test I failed. The square of loose-leaf paper landed between a plate of Wonder Bread and a bowl of homemade salsa.

I stared at the note folded in eighths. I wanted to snatch it up, roll it into a ball, and swallow it. I quickly studied the situation. Everything led back to the boy from earlier. Could he have been El Sapo? Did the mud balls spell some kind of message? What did "c/s" mean?

My brother reached for the note, but my mom was quicker. She put it back in her pocket, saving the evidence for later.

The sun was setting behind our house, where minutes away the Río Grande separated us from another country. Light swam through our wallpapered kitchen and made it even more orange. I would've given almost anything to be somewhere else at that moment.

"C'mon, let's have it, whatever it is," my dad said, raking his fork through the mashed potatoes.

"Okay, but it's not my fault," I said and put both elbows on the table for some balance. "There are these guys at school. VLK. They're a gang."

I took a breath and saw that my brother appeared as excited as when we watched Mil Mascaras, our favorite wrestler, on Mexican TV.

"They wanted to mess me up," I continued, "but nothing happened."

I craved hearing something other than dogs barking outside, so I kept talking. "I found the note in my locker. And at first I couldn't read it—it's written in cholo—but I figured it out. I understand now."

My brother smacked me on the head. "You and that cholo stuff. I told you it was dumb, menso."

"Hey." My dad punctuated his only word by spearing a rectangle of meat loaf.

"And I don't know the boy you caught. He's not El Sapo, is he?" I said to my mom, who hadn't eaten very much off her plate.

"What boy?" my dad said before biting into his meat loaf.

"The one mom made wash windows." I sat up in my chair, happy that I was the only one with answers.

My dad and brother simultaneously turned to my mom.

"He—has—a—girlfriend." There were long pauses between each of my mom's words. As much was said in the silence as in the joining of consonants and vowels.

She might as well have hit me with a broom. Across the head. On my butt. A blow to my stomach.

I burped and tasted salsa. Although I knew it wouldn't help things, all I could do was chew another slice of Wonder Bread. No stories about cholos or mud balls could hide my secret. Ana Garza and I were kissing.

That night, with my ear to the wall, I listened as my mom told my dad about the note she'd found in my pants. She went on and on how I was too young to be kissing girls. How maybe I should go back to Father Yermo. How I was still her "mijito." From a recent conversation I'd eavesdropped on, I remembered her saying the same thing after a trip to Kmart. She'd been upset that I'd asked her to wait in the car while I shopped for school clothes on my own.

My stomach grumbled when I heard her mention my low grades. They agreed that I would be grounded.

I also heard my mom tell my dad about the boys mud-balling our house. She'd intended to scare them off with the broom. Running barefoot, she was so mad that she managed to catch the slowest one. When she asked him why they did it, he said nothing. She even questioned him in Spanish. *Nada*—the boy wasn't giving anything up.

I might've tried my cholo vocabulary, the one I'd been studying off walls and on the bus. "C'mon, don't be a pinche. Why you messing up our house, ése?"

The next day at school I searched the hallways, cafeteria, playground, and even the detention room for the boy my mom had caught. I was bigger than he was. I could get him to confess. I would offer my mom his answers as a bribe to let me go to Western Playland. When I didn't find the boy, I described him to Santiago, making sure to mention that his khakis weren't creased. Santiago said that he sounded like every boy on his side of the barrier.

After the mud balls, my mom finding the note, and my grounding, I tried not to get in any more trouble. Days went by without me seeing much of Ana Garza. When she asked why I couldn't go to Western Playland, I said my mom was sick. I didn't like lying, but I didn't want to tell Ana Garza that my mom had found out we were kissing.

Santiago also stopped coming to my house after I told him about my mom's use of a broom. I assured him that it didn't hurt, remembering the swats I'd gotten for asking about a Spanish word I'd read on the school bus. While I still wasn't sure what "*pendejo*" meant in English, I crowded my mouth with *o*'s. Cholo. Joto. Pendejo.

I would've preferred that my mom hit me again, rather than keep me grounded. I made sure to wash the dishes without being told. Even on nights when it was my brother's turn. I almost hoped I would catch someone throwing mud balls at our house, so I could prove that I was on her side. I made sure to keep the front curtains open, the glass Windexed.

One evening, after I'd hurried home and done my homework, I went to see what my mom was making for dinner. Since I'd been spending all my free time shooting baskets, I hadn't helped her like I used to. In our La Loma home, I'd learned how to clean the beans before you put them in the pot, how much cilantro to put in arroz, and which chiles were the hottest, and best, for salsa.

Without saying anything, I began grating cheese while she diced onions for red enchiladas. We stood right next to each other—hip to hip. Her favorite novela, *Semillas de Amor y Dolor,* played on the TV in the other room. The voices in Spanish were much more dramatic than anything I understood on the school bus. When I heard my mom sniffle, I checked to see if she was crying. She pointed to the onions. We smiled.

"Do you have a lot of homework this weekend?" she asked, adding the onions to the rice.

I wanted to ask why but said, "Not so much."

"Good. There's a company picnic," she said as she took out a pan. The flame of the burner went from blue to orange. Melted lard sizzled when she dropped a spoonful of beans.

I imagined a park filled with old people eating bologna sandwiches and potato salad. When I didn't say anything, she said, "It's at Western Playland. You can bring your friend. What's his name?"

"Santiago." I grinned and inhaled the heavy smell of refried beans. Hungrier than I'd been in weeks, I thought about checking for mangoes but snatched a palmful of Jack cheese instead. I swished the mini orange ball into my mouth.

›› With things at home back to normal, I tried to do the same with my life at school. I was ready to tell Ana Garza the whole story. From the mud balls to me and my mom making up. I wrote it out in my journal, taking my time to stay within the lines, and hoped that it would get me and Ana Garza kissing again. That's what I wanted more than anything.

When I opened my locker the next day, I found a note. I hesitated unfolding it, but the letters were round cursive, not stilted print. Ana Garza's, not a cholo's. I read the note while I made my way outside the school building. The last bell let me know that I'd missed my bus.

"Do you mean it?" These were the first words I said when I met Ana Garza outside by the portable classrooms. She brushed her hair back and avoided eye contact. I dropped my gym bag and tried to take her hand. She slipped it in her rear pocket.

"Yeah, I'm pretty sure."

"Why? Because I didn't walk you to your bus?"

No matter how many steps I moved forward, she kept dancing back.

"No. Not just that—"

"What? What did I do?"

Before she could answer, I started blabbering. Not from the beginning straight to the present like I'd prepared in my journal. My spinning thoughts mixed up my neatly written sentences. "This boy—my mom had a broom—the barrier—do you know El Sapo?—she's not mad anymore—he's a cholo—wanna go to a picnic?"

The words poured out of my mouth like a mudslide. I couldn't escape.

Ana Garza lifted her head. Although she looked in my eyes for the first time, something far away had her attention.

That's when I knew. I just did. The way she kept her hips out of reach. The way she turned her shoulders. The way she sucked in her lips.

Even in her paper-soft voice, the news was bad. She left nothing out. How he put his arm around her. On the El Bandido Roller Coaster. How he kissed her. In the Haunted House. How it just happened. At Western Playland. How I shouldn't be mad.

Mad? I wasn't mad. I wasn't anything. My body was numb. Jell-O. My heart, the fruit trapped inside.

When Ana Garza breathed his name, I wanted to swallow the syllables that grazed her lips. There wasn't a kiss big enough.

Before she could say "Santiago" again, I grabbed my gym bag and took off. My feet pumped under me and my arms flailed at my sides. I ran fast, like I'd imagined I would if a cholo ever came after me.

I sprinted down North Loop Road, a dust devil racing me. The wind smelled like yellow chile. The sun was a giant Spalding beginning its descent.

I crossed Zaragoza Road and kept running. When I reached the canal that ran behind my house, I thought about throwing my gym bag—filled with books, my journal, Ana Garza's note, a mango, and half a peanut butter sandwich—in the algae-colored water, but its weight kept me anchored to the caliche road. I didn't stop running till I arrived at Desert Vista. Even then, I walked fast through our neighborhood with my head tilted back. I couldn't open my mouth wide enough to replace all the air escaping my lungs.

Through the front windows of my house, I saw my mom in the kitchen. She moved her hips side to side. I thought she might've been dancing, like they often did on her novelas, but I realized she was sweeping. I considered going in, grabbing the broom, and telling her I was chasing a cholo.

Like when I'd discover a note in my locker, my heart began running a hundred-yard dash. Blood rushed through my arms and legs. When I ran out of sidewalk, I climbed the graffiti-covered barrier for the first time. Straddling the top rail, I hesitated. When I glanced back, I couldn't tell which was my house. They all appeared the same. I took a deep breath and jumped to the other side.

Busted Big Wheels. Crooked swing sets. Kids in diapers. The houses on this side weren't much different than the ones on the other side except that there seemed to be more things out front. No basketball courts. No birdbaths. No mulberry trees.

I expected to see the boy my mom had caught. I wasn't mad at him, but I knew that I could easily hit him. The fists I carried were heavy.

After going up and down unfamiliar streets—waving to Mary Rodarte, who was in my history class, smelling caldo de res from an open window, hearing a TV switch from Spanish to English to Spanish—I gave up trying to find the right house. I was almost glad that I didn't know where Santiago lived. Although I wasn't sure what I would say, I did know that I wanted to foul him, like if he was going in for a layup. Hard enough so that he would know how bad it felt to not be kissing Ana Garza.

I was resting under a Stop sign, worrying that I should get home before it got dark, when a truck drove by. The Chevy was faded green, made lots of noise, and a ladder hung out the back. None of these was what drew me.

REYES ROOFING. The red letters painted across the doors lifted me off the ground. I followed the truck. My calves were sore, and my gym bag weighed my shoulders down as I ran.

I stopped outside the front gate where the truck had parked. In the driveway, there was a beat-up car. An engine hung by a chain over an open hood, a gaping mouth ready to swallow. A toolbox, wrenches, and sockets—scattered like puzzle pieces—also sat in the oil-stained driveway.

Even with a basketball court and trimmed bushes, this wouldn't have compared to my house. One side of the roof was missing shingles and appeared ready to cave in. The front door was more rust than any color of paint. I couldn't tell where the cement driveway ended and the grassless yard began. Trash and tumbleweeds clenched the chainlink fence.

Before I realized what I was doing, I jumped over the fence and landed in the yard. On my hands and knees, I couldn't remember Santiago saying whether they had dogs.

A few seconds passed. I stood. Looked around. No one.

Still not sure what I was doing, I unzipped my gym bag and reached inside.

I pictured this house like someone—a stranger, a cholo, an ex-best friend—had pictured ours: as a target.

Like kissing Ana Garza for the first time, I knew that if I thought about it too much I would chicken out.

I planted my feet. I inhaled.

I lifted my arm. I focused.

I twisted my hips. I couldn't miss.

As I leaned forward and released, a stream of air brushed my face. On Santiago's front door bloomed the ripe kiss of a mango.

>>> *Good Time* <<<

Peña wasn't exactly sure how he ended up here. A moment ago he was telling his friends that he'd better head home—Marcela would be waking him up early, even though it would be a Saturday and all—and the next thing he knew he was behind the wheel of his truck. A '66 Chevy he'd been fixing up since high school.

In the Good Time Store near Ysleta High School, the fluorescent lights made him squint, his eyeballs bloodshot for sure. Two of his friends, Turi, and his primito, Shorty, were out in the truck counting the money they'd collected. The rest of their Friday night gang back at "the Trees" claimed they were too broke for another case. They dumped out their pockets for cuartos—Busch, Natural Light, or whatever was on sale.

"Hey, why don't you have hot dogs?" Peña asked the cashier behind the counter. He was eyeing a *Penthouse* and hadn't looked up to see who'd walked in the door.

Peña pointed to the words on the front window. HOT DOGS 3 FOR $1. When he walked up to the counter, close enough to grab the cashier, he saw that the guy didn't have a name tag clipped onto his yellow vest, only a smiley face, the store's logo. Peña figured that his sorry ass hadn't worked here long enough to earn a name tag. While Peña wasn't satisfied with his job at Farah Manufacturing, he liked that his last name was stitched on his work shirt. No matter if it was in smaller letters under the company's name. It was as good as "Peña" stamped on the back of a jersey. And that's what all his good friends had always called him.

"Don't worry, I'm not going to rob you. Shit, I'm just hungry," Peña said, still pointing to the front window. HOT DOGS 3 FOR $1. The cashier slipped into the store's back room.

Too hungry to see if the Good Time Man was going to put out any hot dogs, Peña would have to accept nachos as a substitute. He liked the Good Time. The self-serve idea of convenience stores, which were replacing the tienditas all over Ysleta, meant that you took as much as you could for one price. And they're open twenty-four hours.

He pushed the knob on the cheese machine, a Play-Doh yellow stream fell over the tostadas. Although they gave him the shits, he piled on jalapeño slices.

Turi and Shorty finally entered the store.

"Cabrones, what took you? Can you believe there's no hot dogs?" Peña's thumb flattened the red knob, and cheese ran down the counter onto the floor. He pretended not to notice and felt good that the cashier would have some work to do later on.

Turi and Shorty said they'd taken a piss, which put it in Peña's mind that he also had to go. He tossed a crumpled dollar bill on the counter, not caring if the nachos cost more than the hot dogs. That's all he was paying. The cashier stood a safe distance behind the counter. Turi left a wad of bills and coins for a case and the cuartos.

"Get your ass over here," Peña yelled at Shorty, who'd surely swiped something for his munchies.

"Later," Peña said to the Good Time Man before he left the store. "Do your pinche job. Get out some hot dogs." Like that, muy tough guy.

Turi, Shorty, and Peña headed out of the Good Time. Their stroll, like their beer, nice and cool.

Outside the store, Peña busted up at just how full of shit he was. Marcela always told him that he gets to be such an asshole when he drinks. Like tonight. He was glad that she wasn't here to remind him of this. And for other reasons too.

He put the nachos in his truck and hurried to the side of the store. Head dropped back, he pissed all over a Dumpster. The store's name and smiley face redone by many cans of graffiti. Dumb-ass cholillos, he thought, running his eyes over the store's wall, also tattooed with spray paint. At least he used to be able to read this shit. Now who knows what the fuck they're trying to say?

A cop car cruised by on Alameda. A too familiar sight in Ysleta. Peña thought that they might turn around and get on his ass, but they kept on going.

He zipped up as he walked to his truck. The store's street sign— a large smiley face—was a second moon in the sky. An omen for the rest of the night. He cocked his head at the smiley face, as if it was an old friend.

Steering and eating wasn't going to work. He'd already dropped most of the nachos on his jeans and work shirt. Turi grabbed a chip, and a sloppy jalapeño spilled on the upholstery. "Fuck, she's gonna bitch me out." Peña didn't want to clean up in the morning before Marcela's doctor's appointment, so he pitched the nachos out the window. A streak of cheese traced itself along the driver's side of the truck.

Turi handed Peña an open beer and told him to chill. The radio was switched on "the Q," the border city's only rock station among a world of Spanish and Tejano stations. Peña was bobbing his head to Led Zeppelin's "Kashmir," about to take a drink, when Turi let out a warning: "Trucha, cops."

The three of them sat up. Peña passed his beer to Turi, who wedged it under the seat. In the rearview mirror, Peña saw the cop in the passenger seat talking into his radio. A bad sign. Peña thought about reaching for his seat belt but didn't want to throw off his rhythm. The needle of the speedometer danced near 35, what he guessed to be the speed limit.

The cop car stayed close along the familiar drag of Alameda— from Ysleta High past the Hamburger Hut to Zeke's Meat Market. No one in the truck said shit. Peña clicked off the radio when a Bon Jovi song came on. Marcela was the one who liked that joto.

Turi managed to shove most of the beer under the seat, but there were still the open bottles. A big fine. And the pot.

Shorty, alert for the first time tonight, busted out a baggie from under his Oakland Raiders cap. He opened the glove compartment hoping for a hiding place. Peña objected: "You stupid? Don't do that shit."

Shorty had no choice but to cram the baggie down the front of his pants. Peña wanted to laugh at the pendejo, knowing that the cops always searched your bolas, but he told himself to concentrate. He couldn't afford to be pulled over again. Marcela would surely leave his ass in the can this time. She'd been pissed when he woke her up that 3:30 A.M. What made it worse was that he was still a little buzzed when he called her. Nothing he said had made any sense.

Although he'd already paid her back the bail money, he still felt that he owed her. Well, he did, since she'd given him some of her savings to get his truck painted and half of the cost of the new upholstery. She said it was a gift, but he knew better. Thinking about his past made him more nervous about the cops, and he turned his attention back to his driving. He didn't need to look in the mirror to know the cops were still there. The chota's breath thick on his neck.

Coming to the Mission, the intersection of Alameda and Zaragoza, where a light had been green for a good while, Peña debated whether to speed up or slow down.

He was about to gun it, take the yellow, when at the last moment he braked. Strapped in their seat belts, Turi and Shorty rocked forward and back. Their heads snapped against the rear window. They spat cuss words as beer bottles rocketed from under the seat.

At the red light, hands locked on the steering wheel, Peña was a mannequin in the driver's seat. He faced the black river of Alameda. The cop car drifted into the lane on the driver's side.

Peña fought his want to check out the cops. C'mon, damn light, turn green, he said to himself. Don't look over, don't do it. The more he thought about it, the more he had to. Like partying with his friends every Friday even if Marcela made it out to be a big deal.

He took a chance. Real cool. Como nada.

His anxiety of getting hauled in was replaced by disgust when he saw the officer in the passenger seat. Even with a crew cut and goatee, uniform and badge, Leo Valdez was still the dick who'd made Peña's years at Ysleta High much more of a pain in the ass than the last mile.

In the three years since their graduation, they'd only seen each other a few times, but the stare they held was intense. As if they'd just bumped shoulders in the hall. Leo turned to the gringo officer driving, said something Peña couldn't hear, and turned back to face him. The high school rivals threw each other stares while saying nothing.

Peña was about to say, "What the fuck?" when the cop car's sirens came alive. The white ship sailed away. Right through the red light. Muy chingón. Flashing lights streaked patriotic colors all over Ysleta's fruit stands and llanterías and pawnshops.

"Ah, hell. Of all the cops," Peña said.

Turi and Shorty, who'd been quiet all this time, cracked up and fished the beer out from under them.

"Shit, that dude had you by the balls," Turi said, grabbing himself between the legs.

"Fuck that. I don't know why that guy sweats me."

"No te hagas. You know he's got a hard-on for Marcela."

"Fuck, that was at the High."

"Doesn't he know she's your old lady now?"

"She's just crashing with me, you know, while her mom's pissed at her."

"You guys are all Love Boat a la chingada."

"Cállate, cabrón. Give me my birria."

"Fucking puto thinks he's all bad." Shorty pulled the baggie out from his crotch.

"Don't play with yourself, pelado," Turi said to Shorty.

Laughter filled the truck.

Peña pushed in a cassette, making sure to place a matchbook in the player or else it would eat another of Marcela's tapes. He cranked the volume. Heavy drumbeats and biting guitar riffs screamed out of the Bronco Swap Meet speakers. Noticing that the light had gone from green to yellow about to turn red again, he peeled out.

The truck coasted down Alameda, cruising back to a good time.

>>> Handling the ride of one of the Lower Valley's many canal roads, the open beer between his legs spitting up, Peña searched for the bonfire. One of the reasons he and his friends hung out at the Trees was that it was hidden from the heavy Border Highway traffic less than a mile away. The helicopters above—the ever-present migra—were too busy watching for mules or coyotes, drug and wetback smuggling being big business this close to the Río.

Peña wondered if the rest of the gang had bailed or if they'd just let the fire die. Although the night was getting cooler, none of his drunk-ass friends would've bothered to round up any wood. The place was littered with branches from the many dried cotton-woods. When Peña got out of the truck, he saw that the only ones here were Benny and the Apache Brothers. They said the rest of the gang gave up on him, Turi, and Shorty ever returning. The cuartos Turi passed around made everyone even happier to see each other. Peña caught up with the Apache Brothers, who he hadn't seen for a few Fridays. Turi and Benny joined Shorty with his baggie of treats.

"So, this is the new tow truck." Peña shook hands with Alex and Poncho.

"Simón. ¿Qué piensas?" Alex replied.

"It sure the hell beats that damn Ford. Damn, a tow truck that needed a tow," Peña said. "Did you junk that piece of crap?"

"Naw, it's still in the garage," Alex said.

"Esa troquita's an antique," Poncho added.

"Hell, it's like the one Fred Sanford drives," Peña said.

They laughed.

"¿Te gusta?" Alex turned around to show Peña the back of his windbreaker—a picture of an Indian, Geronimo or somebody, above Old English lettering: LOS HERMANOS APACHE, INC.

"We might set you up si te portas bien," Poncho said.

"Jackets y todo. What's the 'Inc.' for?" Peña asked.

"Hell, we don't know. We thought it sounded good. Like in the phone book."

"I guess it could be la jefita," Poncho said as he read the back of his brother's jacket. "We hate all that office shit. It's too much like school."

"We like real work, ése. Something you huevones wouldn't know about." Alex flexed his biceps. Peña was impressed that the brothers hadn't lost any of their linebacker strength. While Peña felt that he, too, busted his ass at Farah Manufacturing—unload-ing and loading crates of fabric, thread, and trim—he'd let himself go since he'd graduated. As evidence, his gut hung over his belt buckle, a brass Chevy emblem.

Peña walked around the tow truck and admired its newness. EL PERRO NEGRO, as stenciled on the doors, was a symbol of hard work. As much as he liked fixing up his truck, he'd rather buy himself a new ride. Doing one thing at a time—a paint job, tires and rims, the upholstery—was more Marcela's idea than his. He knew that's the way it would be with everything if she got him to marry her. One thing at a time—a house, furniture, kids, trading his truck in for a station wagon or some shit.

In no time at all, the gang killed off the cuartos. With their arms outstretched, palms open and ready, the case in Peña's truck was passed around. They leaned against the trucks, bullshitting. Occasionally, one left the group to get closer to the smoldering embers. Everyone said it was too cold for this time of year. They seemed surprised, although they'd lived all their lives in this desert town.

Peña stepped away from the group once Turi brought up the cops catching up with them. The gang cracked up at how Leo always got the best of Peña. Benny, who'd made a failed play for Marcela at the High, was the loudest and made Peña feel that he should just head out.

Who needs this shit? he thought as he went behind a crippled tree to take a piss. Loud laughter mixed with the semi trucks speeding down the Border Highway. Peña couldn't get Leo's mug out of his mind. The earlier run-in with the pig had fucked up his mood real good. Friday, his one night to party—Marcela not around—and the crap that he thought he'd left in the past had snuck up on him.

While he was close to his camaradas—guys he'd known for years, played sports and raised hell with—nothing had been the same since he and Marcela hooked up. So much shit came with dating one of the hottest chicks in Ysleta, and he often wondered if it was even worth it.

A helicopter passed overhead. He flipped it off. In his mind, la migra was worse than the cops. At least the cops only busted you. They didn't throw your ass back to the place you were trying to leave.

He farted and clutched his gut. Something awful stirred inside. He didn't know if it was the beer and jalapeños or everything else that he'd ingested this night.

"What you doing over here, cabrón?" Turi crept up on Peña.

"Pissing, fucker. Want to see how big it is?" Peña offered.

"You wish, joto. Your chile's a Pequin. Mine's long and hot."

They cracked up.

"Shit, it's cold," Peña said and zipped up.

"You're not taking off, are you?"

Peña shrugged.

"Benny asked me if you and Marcela were still shacking up."

"Fuck 'em. And that puto cop too."

"C'mon, those vatos just like giving you shit."

"All those cabrones need to—"

"Check it out, ése, your ruca gives us all hard-ons."

Peña wanted to lie: That he was done with Marcela. That she didn't go on about getting married. That she wasn't late this month.

He said nothing. And it bothered him that he couldn't share any of this with Turi, his oldest friend.

"Chale, she's more of a pain in the ass than a hard-on."

"Don't sweat it. Grab another birria before those culeros drink it all."

As a yellow moon remained on guard, the group's good time, like the fire, died out with the last of the beers. Turi followed Benny to some güera's party on the other side of I-10, near Eastwood High School. Shorty asked Peña for a ride home. They hung back with the Apache Brothers.

In just a T-shirt, Peña was cold, so he fetched his high school letterman jacket from his truck. Although the maroon and white jacket no longer buttoned around his gut, it was the warmest one he owned. A "Y" was stitched on the chest and All-District Basketball and All-City Baseball patches on the sleeves. They reminded everyone, including himself, of the high school athlete he used to be.

He went over next to Shorty, who was listening to Alex tell a story that they'd all heard before. It was of the time they broke into the High and took Ysleta's mascot, a wooden Indian named Kawliga.

"We were going to drop it in the canal and see if it floated to the pinche Río," Alex said. "But we couldn't figure out how to get it out of the building."

"The chingadera was heavy. I thought his head was going to bust off," Poncho added.

It had been Peña's idea to dump it in the faculty rest room.

"Now I know why they have that damn Indio locked up." Shorty was the only one still trying to finish up at the High. "Because of you pinche locos."

"What were we drinking?" Peña asked while everyone cracked up over that night, which could've easily been yesterday. Or tonight. All that was missing was a stolen key.

The Apache Brothers were heading to Chico's Tacos. Peña said that he had to take Shorty home and get on his way too. Not wanting Alex and Poncho to give him shit that Marcela had him by the short hairs, he took out the cuarto that he'd hidden. The gift sent the brothers on their way.

"Next Friday," one of them said.

"Simón," the rest answered.

>>> In the truck, Shorty told Peña that he didn't want to go home. "Wanna cruise and finish this?" Shorty busted out a half-smoked joint. Peña hesitated before telling him that he better call it a night, he was tired and had to wake up early. The image of Marcela waiting in the front of his mind.

Shorty said that was cool, but if he could do him a favor. Instead of going home, Shorty wanted to be dropped off at this chick's house. Ronnie was her name. He'd met her at Ascarate Park. Peña checked his gas gauge, the red needle playing over the E. Shorty's want to get some made Peña grin. He nodded as he passed up a gas station, figuring he'd stop on his way home. Before getting on the Border Highway, Shorty complained that he had to take a leak, so they pulled over. Peña stood next to Shorty on the curb, trails of piss streaming in the street. A streetlight flickered its envy of the moon.

Shorty broke the silence: "Peña, why'd you quit?"

Peña didn't answer, not immediately knowing what Shorty was talking about.

After a few seconds, Peña realized where he'd pulled over, the dead-end street behind Ysleta High School. The Tribe's baseball field rested before them, dark and empty.

"I didn't quit," Peña answered. "I'd had enough."

"What do you mean? You stopped playing before your senior year, no?"

"Yeah, well." Peña cut his answer short and approached the chainlink fence that surrounded the High.

"With you and Rene Ponce pitching and Gilbert Medina hitting cleanup, híjola, you guys were gonna kick ass."

"Damn, Shorty, you remember more than I do." Peña clutched the fence and stared beyond the field. The school building stood in the background. A mountain he'd climbed but whose shadow he couldn't escape.

"Te dejabas cae." Shorty struggled to zip up his pants and finally just tightened his belt.

"Fuck, I don't know about all that." A short pause. "But on this field nothing mattered—not even all those pinche stickers."

"After you quit, those putos from Eastwood and Hanks kicked our asses. Those gringos are calotes."

"You know why?"

"Naw, ése."

"It's cause en el otro lado"—he pointed toward left field, north, beyond I-10—"they don't eat beans every day."

"Simón. Those rich cabrones eat at Luby's or some shit."

They both cracked up.

"You know what I remember most?"

"What?"

"Marcela yelling."

"I know. The other team always stared. Fuck it, she flipped them off."

"She's got some lungs." Peña smiled and added, "She still yells, but only when I'm in trouble. Like tonight. She's gonna bitch me out for sure. Let's get outta here."

Before they got back in the truck, Shorty again asked, "So, why'd you quit?"

Peña thought about telling Shorty what only Marcela and he knew—that he had to. She'd told him that she was pregnant, so he'd quit the team and got a job, the one he still had at Farah Manufacturing. She ended up saying it was a false alarm. But by that time he couldn't go back, since Coach Beltrán was really pissed off when he left the team. Peña never even turned in his uniform. #12 was still somewhere in his closet along with his cleats.

After going over the speed limit on the Border Highway, Peña took the Delta Exit and followed Shorty's directions to Ronnie's house.

Under a busted streetlight, no dogs barking, Peña put his truck in neutral and left it running.

Wanting to be the one to ask questions, he put the squeeze on Shorty. "So, you and this ruca getting it on?"

"Naw, we've come close, pero tú sabes." A big smile crept up his face. "Maybe tonight."

"Do it." He gave Shorty a light shove. "Hit a home run. You can't get enough of those."

They shook hands, their fists locked for a second at the end. The young carnal jumped out of the truck and hustled across a grass lawn, as if leaving the batter's box.

Peña cruised east on Alameda, heading home, with thoughts of yanking off his Tony Lamas and climbing into bed. If he was lucky, Marcela would already be snoring, and he could sleep off the night without them fooling around. He would never tell her this, since she would take it wrong. After years of doing it, she often accused him of getting bored with her. He'd told her she was crazy. Although, sometimes when he was inside of her, his thoughts were of the women he flirted with at work.

The rhythms of Santana drove him past the speed limit. A street of green lights and no cops made the ride that much more chingón. He cruised Alameda like he owned it.

Near Yarbrough, two traffic lights past Riverside High School, he was drumming on the dash when the cassette got stuck. "Fucking shit." He cussed some more when the truck also started to sputter. The red needle of the gas gauge had moved way to the left of the E. The truck farted to a stop between I&M Plumbing and the Bronco Ballroom/Swap Meet/Bingo Parlor.

Hands shoved in his jacket pockets and cold air on his face, he walked down the canal road parallel to Alameda. He wanted to be pissed at someone other than himself. Turi, for making him go on a beer run. Shorty, for having him drive all the way to his chick's. Marcela, for never putting gas in after her night classes. Walking for a long time, he knew that it was nobody's fault but his own. The sign in his sight seemed to agree.

The smiley face of the Good Time Store was a beacon. When he walked into the bright space of the store this time around, he wasn't in such a pumped-up mood. He was relieved to see a woman behind the counter, not the man from earlier. Peña didn't remember what he'd said, but chances were that he'd been an asshole.

He greeted the woman. "R. Piñeda," read her name tag. Maybe

she'd been a cheerleader who'd graduated before him. He smiled and asked her if they had a gas can he could borrow. She said she'd look in the back room.

Feeling a little better now, he realized that he was also running on empty. In the rear of the store, he spotted the Grande Guzzler. The 44-ounce cup that he filled with soda had a smiley face printed on it, like everything else in the store. This smiley face had a long bigote and sombrero. Pancho Villa or some shit. Peña cracked up even more when he glanced down the self-serve counter. He wasn't hungry, and his stomach still wasn't right, but he had to go for it. HOT DOGS 3 FOR $1. Before he could swipe on mustard and relish, pour on melted cheese and jalapeños, he heard voices coming from behind the counter.

He almost dropped his Grande Guzzler when he saw the cashier from earlier. Peña tried to be real cool and walked up to the counter. He hoped the Good Time Man wouldn't remember him. No way. The guy turned to his fellow cashier and mumbled something before carrying away the gas can. "R. Piñeda" shrugged and seemed sorry.

Peña bolted out of the store and leaned against a wall, ignoring the graffiti that outlined him. No messages—past or present— mattered now. All he cared about was getting his truck, driving home, sleeping.

His options were few: Call Turi, who was probably still partying somewhere, or walk home and pick up the truck in the morning. Or maybe Los Hermanos Apache would tow it. Whichever scenario Peña thought of, the bottom line was how Marcela would react.

The last time he stayed out late she'd waited a few days before yelling at him. He'd hoped that she wouldn't notice the scratches on the truck. Of course, he'd lied and not confessed racing down a canal road lined with trees, thorned branches for fingernails.

After the same bad thoughts spiraled over and over in his head, the last ounce of this Friday night's good time was pissed away. He decided he'd call Marcela. She could walk down the block and borrow her mom's car. He'd rather be bitched out now than in a few hours. The clock inside the store—another damn smiley face—told him it was only a few hours till dawn.

Before he reached the pay phone, a car pulled up to the store. He recognized it. There wasn't another souped-up, black-and-gold Trans Am in Ysleta.

It belonged to "Officer Poncherelo," Peña's nickname for Leo ever since he joined the police force and scored his new ride. "L. Valdez," as his officer's badge read, stepped out of his Trans Am. A chick sat in the passenger seat. Peña couldn't see in the tinted windows if she was someone he knew.

"What's up, Peña?" Officer Valdez asked as if nothing.

"Q-vo," Peña muttered.

"How's it going?"

"All right, you know."

"Yeah, ése."

The words passed as quickly as the cop did into the convenience store. Peña tried to blow it off as more bad luck and dropped a quarter into the pay phone. Stranded at the Good Time felt worse knowing that he was going to wake up Marcela.

One ring. Two rings. "C'mon, babes, pick up." Three rings.

"Hey, Peña. Tocayo, that your truck on Alameda?"

Peña turned, the receiver still on his ear. He held the phone down to his side, thought of many wiseass remarks for this cabrón, insults that would get him out of his face, but all he said was, "Simón."

He said nothing else as "Ponch" went to his Trans Am and opened his trunk. He stood by the phone. His body slouched over, eyes bleary, palms sweaty—like a batter down to his last strike.

Leo walked up to him and placed a gas can at his feet. When Leo patted him on the sleeve, his hand cupping a baseball, he took notice of the policeman's patches. They were like tattoos of who and what his rival had become.

Leo told him that he could get the can back to him when he had a chance. He waited till Leo got back in his car before he reached for the gas can.

When he realized that he still held the receiver, he put it to his ear. "¿Quién es? ¿Quién es?" He was tempted to yell back at Marcela, but he hung up just as she started cussing.

With a dollar's worth of gas, he walked away from the Good Time. The sign's giant smiley face cast a yellow glow down on him. It pissed him off. His final wish for the night was to knock down the sign, use the pole for a bat, and hit the hell out of the smiley face. Over the Border Highway. Past the Río. Home run.

>>> *Amoroza Tires* <<<

>>> <<<

The layers of graffiti were a sign that Amoroza Tires had been closed for a long period. The names of gangs, their members, and their crossed-out rivals almost completely covered the side of the cinder-block building.

VLK c/s   El Chuco ATM   Indio PV
Muna y Sapo   ~~LOS FATHERLESS~~

Before Tony Amoroza opened the three padlocks that secured his shop, he checked to see if the surrounding businesses had also been targeted. On the right, the Zaragoza Bakery was almost free of spray-painted messages. The mural of children eating Mexican sweet bread was left untouched. The 24-hour Deluxx Car Wash & Laundromat on the left of the tire shop was a different story. Los Kennedys had also used the wash stalls as canvases. The collages of old and new graffiti faced the heavy traffic on Zaragoza Road.

Although Tony had anticipated plenty of work on his first day back, he was bothered that he was already behind. He had to push six flat tires out of the way before he could raise the large metal sheets that covered the front doors and windows. Two of the flats were badly worn. He'd repaired them many times before. The plugs of rubber he'd used to patch up the tires stuck out of the threads like blackheads. He thought it a waste of time to repair the tires. And if he felt La Señora Herida could afford it, he'd try and sell her some hardly used ones.

Whichever neighbor had left the other tires had done it as an act of faith that Tony would return to work. His wife, María de Dolores Amoroza, had passed away last week after months in the hospital.

The morning light coming through the tire shop's windows revealed a cement floor covered in trash. He had to step over pieces of rubber, aluminum and metal cans, pages of newspaper, and piles of dirt from the surrounding Chihuahua Desert. Rather than search for the broom that was thrown in the back, he kicked the debris into a corner. Clouds of dust floated in squares of brown light. He coughed more than once to clear his throat.

In these first minutes of being back in his shop, he was confronted by regret. While he'd spent the last weeks, especially the days since the funeral, telling his daughters, Ramona and Pima, that they had to be strong, he now questioned his own will.

He choked back his remorse by retreating into the routine that he'd nurtured over the years. In the tire shop's back room, he put down his lunch bag, sat on a makeshift bench, and unlaced his shoes. From a nail, he snatched his work overalls and slipped into the coarse fabric that sagged on his short frame. He plopped a beat-up El Paso Diablos baseball cap on his head. Before he finished lacing up his work boots—a gray-black like the tools and equipment scattered around the tire shop—he heard someone pulling into the gravel driveway. Peeking out the front door, he recognized the truck as belonging to Mando, his compa's teenage son. Hard rock music poured out of his windows. Tony shook his head and worried his girls would ever be so loud. He hoped not.

"Qué onda," Mando said, stepping out of his truck. He wore torn jeans and a concert T-shirt with the sleeves ripped off, a tattoo on his right arm. He drove one of these 4x4's raised high off the ground.

From the truck's bed, the teen dumped out a flat tire. Tony put his hand to his back. He was certain that his body would snap at every joint when he lifted the giant tire. But it didn't.

"Gracias a Dios," he mumbled—a habit he had borrowed from his wife, who'd used many sayings in Spanish that invoked God's name. "Que Dios te cuide." "Dios nos bendiga." "Si lo manda Dios." His wife had recited each with an equal amount of conviction, while he said them for the same reason he crossed himself whenever he passed a church—Catholic or not—because he'd witnessed his mother do it all her life.

When he went outside to switch on the electricity, he wanted to keep on walking. The desert stretched for miles behind the tire shop. Endless sand dunes populated with mesquite and cacti invited him to escape. All the lights and outlets seemed to be working.

Back in the tire shop, he strained to raise the tire and separate the heavy wheel from the rim. Mando helped him hold the tire in place and asked if he got a discount. Tony's reply was nonverbal: He wiped the sweat off his brow with a grease-colored rag.

The nail he yanked from the truck's tire was the size of a railroad spike. He sandpapered the inside area around the hole. Next, he spread globs of adhesive that would hold the parche to the rubber. Mando watched curiously. Although this work was second nature to Tony, more often than before he was short of breath and the glue gave birth to a headache.

"Where the hell did you get this?" He held the long nail for Mando to see, almost poking his nostril.

"No se. Me and Placido were out four-wheeling last night." Mando backed off and continued, "Cuando la jefita me despierto para ir downtown, it was bien flat."

Although his compa's son sounded as if he was trying to apologize more than explain, he looked at the teen unforgivingly when he said, "I gave her cambio for the bus."

He snatched a ten-dollar bill from Mando, who kept his hand out for change. After Tony pocketed the money without saying anything, he threw a tire iron at the malcriado's feet and pointed to the jack. Mando lowered his head and rolled the tire to his truck.

In the front room of the tire shop, opposite the wall of sockets, screwdrivers, hammers, and other tools, there was a green vinyl car seat that Tony had salvaged from the county dump. When his wife had asked him what he wanted with that piece of junk, he told her that it was for customers to sit on while they waited. That is, if they didn't mind springs poking their nalgas. She said they would. He didn't care.

His back hurt more now than when he'd awakened. He decided to take a breather before he started on the flat tires left at his doorstep. Lying on his side, his right leg resting on the car seat's armrest, he picked up a stray wad of paper from the ground. The oil-stained page of newsprint was from the *National Enquirer*. Under a black-and-white photograph was a headline in bloody script: BEWARE!! MEXICAN VAMPIRE INVADES U.S.

Although he'd read this particular story many times before, he read it again in case he'd missed any buried details. He remembered the mysterious marks on the necks of children and the emptied carcasses of farm animals but had forgotten about the girl who swore the fanged beast was someone from her town. The quiet laughs he enjoyed made him temporarily forget his aches.

The last time his shop was close to going out of business, his wife had decided it was best if she took over. Among many criticisms, she'd told him that he neglected his customers: "You make them wait so long. If you won't get a soda machine, they should have something to read. Tú sabes, like when you're getting a haircut."

"This is a llantería. Not a library, mujer," he'd said to his wife. "They don't come here for that."

Like with most things in their fifteen-year marriage, she pushed and he gave in to her wishes. On a trip to Big 8 Supermarket, while his wife and daughters did the shopping, he discovered a world of tabloids to choose from. *Star. Globe. Sun. National Enquirer.*

From then on, every week, he purchased the tabloids and brought them to his shop. He read them during slow work periods and when he took time out for lunch. Soon after, he began clipping out the articles that fascinated him the most. The walls of his shop were soon covered in collages of his favorite tales.

Each time his wife asked why he read such nonsense, he wanted to tell her that they helped him forget the responsibilities that often overwhelmed him: running a business, paying the rent, providing for his family. Instead, he simply told her that they were funny, a way to pass the time.

While his wife considered the tabloids nothing more than tonterías, he'd caught her sneaking them into the back office. When his daughters came around the tire shop on weekends, they helped him cut and paste. And his customers enjoyed the wild stories, too, as if Amoroza Tires was their very own art gallery, the only one most knew of in Ysleta.

With the muscles in his lower back relaxing, he dragged over another loose sheet from the floor.

AS BIG AS PLUMS, read the headline in bold letters. FILLED MY

MILK BUCKET MANY TIMES. A Peruvian woman claimed that it rained diamonds while she was gardening one day.

Why can't this happen to me? he asked himself as he skimmed the article. On the back of this page was a photo of a weather-beaten man chugging from a bottle on a beach. MAN SURVIVES DAYS AT SEA: USES CRATE OF CHAMPAGNE AS LIFESAVER. The headline made Tony thirsty. He was positive that he wouldn't last too long surrounded by nothing but water. The thought of being that alone scared him.

He sat up on the vinyl car seat and made a pile of the tabloid stories that had peeled off the walls. The pages were yellowed and crisp like dried cornhusks. Dirt clung to balls of adhesive. Rather than throw the pages out and burn them, as his wife would have certainly done, he thought he could re-paste them on the walls, where a few pages remained. He got down on his hands and knees. His gathering of stories was disrupted by his compa's son peeling out onto Zaragoza Road.

Outside, a dust devil made its way toward the car wash next door. As if warned by the graffiti-covered stalls, he carted the jack to the fenced-in tire yard behind the tire shop. His shoulder sloped down from the weight of the tool.

The tire yard was nothing more than a half acre of desert put to some practical use. Tires of countless sizes and various conditions formed tar-colored mountains. Often, while walking through the tire yard, he would see a rat or a snake scamper from one stack of tires to the next. His unsteady heart would react quicker than any of his limbs. He had put off hauling the tires to the dump, although he'd promised his wife. Now, like so many other things, he would never do it. There was no one to hold him to his word.

"Perro cabrón. If you come back here, I'm going to shoot you." He yelled out at the open land beyond his property, assuming the target of his anger was hiding on the other side of the fence. While the chainlink fence that the previous gringo owner had erected still stood after all these years, the ground below it had given away to wind and rain. The desert changed daily. And whether you liked it or not, you had to change right along with it. Tony knew this.

From the claw marks and shit he'd stepped in, he'd concluded a dog had been doing the digging. He'd done his best to patch up the holes under the tire yard's fence. Garbage can. Cinder blocks. Junked rims. An anvil. Boulders. Tires, tires, tires. It seemed that no matter what he used to plug up the holes, the dog simply dug around it. This left him with few options and less patience.

What made it worse was that he didn't know why he wanted to keep the mugroso animal from coming in the tire yard anyway. It wasn't like the dog was taking anything. There was nothing it could eat, unless it was so hungry that it could digest rubber. And if it was that starved, then maybe he should leave it alone. From living his whole life in the Chihuahua Desert, he appreciated how those with instincts survived.

Straining to roll a tractor tire to block a new hole, he dropped onto the ground. He was tired. The fat sun held him down. His fatigue wasn't purely physical, soreness of his arms and stiffness in his hips, it was also trapped in his organs. His stomach felt like a recycled inner tube. His lungs were overinflated. And he swore to the doctors at the Ysleta Clinic that he could feel his heart's rhythm change with each new emotion. When he didn't feel depressed or sorry for himself, then he was worrying. About his shop, about his health, and most often, about his daughters.

Am I a good father?

This question didn't take root so easily in his mind, but, ultimately, that's what his questions added up to.

Is there milk in the refrigerator?

Will their shoes last through the school year?

And each day there were more questions. Or different faces of the same question. They piled up like the tires in the yard.

His back continued to hurt, and now he thought his chest did too. He reached into his pockets, but without his wife to remind him, he'd forgotten his pills and left them at home. All he found was a piece of bubble gum.

He blew a pink bubble as he left the tractor tire on the ground. The latest hole under the fence would stay. If the dog wants a place to sleep, he thought, then the mugroso can have it. The yard might as well be of some use, not just a cemetery for all these pinche llantas.

WORKER TAMES GOAT-DOG

The morning hours passed with only a few customers stopping by the tire shop. After fixing the flats left at his door, he pasted the recycled tabloid stories on the tire shop's walls. He took his time, smoothing out the sheets and running his fingers over the air bubbles.

While initially he'd posted them randomly, this time he studied them for any possible connections. He assigned groups to each wall. UFO sightings with celebrity scandals. Miracle drugs with strike-it-rich schemes. Cattle mutilations with natural catastrophes. Heroic feats with ghost stories.

He was piecing together a giant puzzle. And although he couldn't say what the big picture might be, he had faith that a message would materialize.

If his wife had been alive, she would've said that he was like the girl who waited weeks for La Virgen to reappear on a water tank in Sparks, the nearby colonia. After the girl kept vigil for months, Bishop Peña had to convince her—and hundreds of believers—to go home. His wife was the one who cut out the *Times* article. He'd added it to his shop's collage despite his doubt of a miracle. A man in Colorado who finds a BABY ALIEN IN RIVER, now that's a miracle, he wanted to say to his wife. But the Catholic child in him, the tattered scapular he wore, kept him from being completely blasphemous.

Mid-afternoon on this first day back, he locked up the tire

shop for a brief period. And while eating a burrito, he drove to the nearby Good Time Store. There certainly wasn't any money to spend on such an expense, so he chose the cheapest bag of dog food. He justified the purchase by imagining this intruder as a good thing. At least that's what his horoscope implied: "Don't ignore signs of luck. Be aware of new faces and names. Keep secrets close to home." As much as the tabloids' slick covers drew his attention, he would wait before he bought anything for himself.

A black dog with long teeth was what he imagined on his drive back to the tire shop. At night he would lock it inside. And it would bark, loud and mean. He had faith in such an animal like his wife had in saints. A watchdog would guarantee that no one would dare break in. This fresh worry was a result of the amount of graffiti that covered his business and the 24-hour Deluxx Car Wash & Laundromat. The cryptic messages were black snakes slithering on the walls.

"Soon enough, we'll crawl inside and take the little that your family has left," the gangs in Ysleta seemed to be warning.

His sudden compassion to welcome the dog was an example of how unsteady he was. In the morning he'd been close to locating his rifle and taking a post atop a pile of tires, staking out the poor animal, but now he thought that he might soon have a pet.

A German shepherd that sat and fetched was his latest image of what the dog would look like. And it would certainly become his loyal companion. Or a Saint Bernard, white and brown with a barrel on its collar, that saved people stranded in the mountains. He'd read about such an incident in the *Star*.

FAMILY RESCUED IN HEART OF DESERT

As the falling sun preyed on those who lived near the river, Tony struggled to mount a patched-up tire. His knees popped like firecrackers when he crouched to tighten the rusted lug nuts. A pain shot up his spine to his neck. It would be impossible to get out of bed tomorrow, he felt in his bones. Hunched over, he took Mrs. Cruz's money without responding to questions if he was all right. He'd swallowed more than enough sympathy.

He wanted to let the community know—maybe by spray-painting his own graffiti at the Ysleta Post Office—that he was hurting, but the worse pain was locked inside his body, secured away like the tools and materials in his aging shop.

In back of the work area, there was a bathroom with barely enough space for a sink and toilet, both of which leaked. Rummaging through the medicine cabinet, he found everything but aspirins. Band-Aids. Jergen's lotion. Flintstones vitamins. Foot powder. Pepto-Bismol. Cough drops. Like the medicine cabinet at home, no near-empty bottle or expired package was ever thrown away. They bunched up in stacks like some kind of a drugstore altar.

A menthol cough drop felt good in his throat. He hoped it would soothe his pains. Massaging his neck with a wet pañuelo, he came out of the bathroom. A door to an adjacent room was slightly open. The room was an office he'd added for his wife. When she'd insisted on managing the tire shop, among many things she'd made it clear that she wanted her space away from the grease and mess.

The office door hung crookedly on its cracked frame and loose hinges. He told himself he should fix it, but that would mean having to remove the door. And he wasn't ready for what rested behind the faded blue wood.

Standing before the door, he kicked the bottom. When he kicked it again, harder this time, the screws popped off the hinges. The door came forward and knocked him on the head. He cussed as he let it slam down on the cement.

A dirty haze lit up the office.

There was a desk, a stack of magazines serving as one of its legs, and a filing cabinet against the far wall. In addition to the desk, the previous owner had left a small refrigerator that hummed a UFO noise when plugged in. Tony's contribution was a crooked stool that he'd salvaged from the county dump.

Sitting down and rubbing his head, he stared at the only other object in the office. On the day his wife had moved in, she had him fetch two rims from the tire yard and stack them in a corner. She placed a soda bottle crate on top and draped a scrap of fabric over it. Atop this makeshift table, an altar appeared.

School pictures of their daughters. Medallitas. Velas. Memorial cards. Family and friends' obituaries. Jars of holy water. A vial of sacred dirt. Rosaries. Milagritos. Satin flowers. Statues of saints. A glow-in-the-dark San Antonio. A wooden Saint Francis clutching a bird's nest. Santa Lucía with a dish of eyeballs. A ceramic San Martín de Porres, a dog at his feet. Santo Niño de Atoche sitting. Another one standing.

The centerpiece of Dolores's altar was a tall statue of Saint Joseph. His wife assured him that this saint would watch over the tire shop. Once he saw how much she trusted San José, he believed her. First thing every morning, his wife had picked up the statue, wiped his face, kissed him, and thanked him for his security. By how dirty he was, it was obvious that no one had been in the room since Tony last shut the office door. On that day, he'd returned from running an errand and found his wife slumped over the desk, one hand clenched in a fist and the other still on the adding machine.

Nailed on the wall behind Dolores's altar was a calendar, of a year long gone, that had been distributed by Cristo Rey Catholic Church. The church's motto—"Mantenga La Fe"—was printed above a picture. La Virgen de Guadalupe stood with her hands outstretched over the Sierra de Juárez. The sun rose behind Her. The bottom right-hand corner of the weathered calendar was ripped. He imagined the Río Grande snaking through the valley below the mountains.

Alone in the office, he stood and walked over to Dolores's altar.

Santo Niño leaned crookedly against a candle. This statue of the Niño, his wife had told him, had been her great-grandmother's. The angel-faced boy came to life and roamed nights performing acts of goodwill. That's why his soles were always worn. Tony didn't exactly believe this. Not only did he find little escape in such Catholic tales, but he thought the Niño looked a lot like Lino, "El Tontito," the dim-witted boy who sold snow cones outside the Bronco Bingo Parlor.

"So, does El Niño pee on himself también?" he'd kidded his wife.

"Show some respect, viejo menso," she'd replied and pinched him.

Wanting a closer look of the statue's innocent face, he picked up El Niño. As quick as a sneeze, it slipped out of his hands. His cussing did little to break the fall of the statue. The pieces littered the floor. Among the remains, the bottom half was the only part left intact.

"What the hell's this?" he said as he knelt and picked up the piece. From the Niño's plaster base, he removed a roll of bills. He had no idea why Dolores's altar hid this money. The five ten-dollar and seven five-dollar bills made him suspicious of how much more was hidden. He inspected each of the statues.

In Saint Francis's arms and legs, he found six twenty-dollar bills. A plastic figure of the Sacred Heart covered a tin can of thirty-eight silver dollars and four Susan B. Anthony coins that he mistook for worthless pesos. Six ten-dollar bills were crushed into the bottom of a burned-out candle.

Eager for more, he dug his fingers in Saint Joseph and felt a wad of bills. But even with some pliers, he couldn't remove the money. Out of respect for his wife, he hesitated before getting a tire iron from the yard.

How else can I get the money? he asked himself while locking the front door.

The loyal San José hid thirteen twenty-dollar bills. Although

Tony felt certain that he would go to hell for it, he said a "Hail Mary" and pretended a porcelain Virgin Mary was a piñata. It shattered as easily as a jar of nails. His prize was a neatly folded fifty-dollar bill.

With his body pains, the intruding dog, and the fallen door temporarily forgotten, he sorted the money and wondered if his wife had considered how much to put in each statue. He wished she was here so he could ask her, but figured, like with so many other things now, that he would have to come up with his own answers.

It's just as well she isn't here, he thought, or else she'd damn me for sure. "A Dios se lo pagaras."

After eating his second burrito, he counted the money again. While it didn't come close to paying his debts, it did begin to buy him some time. He put the money in the grease-stained lunch bag, saved the larger pieces of the statues in the desk, and kicked the leftover debris behind the refrigerator.

No matter how he arranged the remaining items, the pillaged altar looked nothing like what his wife had created. He thought of using the money to buy new statues but realized that wasn't the best thing to do.

"It's not like I'm stealing," he told San José.

The saint's head rested in his palm, solid and silent.

> > >   < < <

Tony was awake but didn't want to open his eyes. As long as he kept them shut, he could pretend it wasn't there. He imagined other things in its place: a recent photo of his family, an Aztec calendar in blue and red stone, one of those velvet paintings sold in Juárez—even a clock would have been better. Only after lying to himself that he would repair it did he open his eyes.

The crack along the wall had grown, about seven inches, since he first noticed it. A certain reminder of how this house was giving way to time. Not even making the sign of the cross, another Catholic habit, could keep him from resenting how much could be taken away.

Still keeping to one side, he threw the covers off and forced himself out of bed. His bones cracked awake with each step to the shower. Although the hot water soothed his back, he reluctantly hurried. More than once, his wife had complained of having to take cold showers. I'll get to it, he'd told her. And now, when his daughters made a fuss, he realized that fixing the faulty water heater was another broken promise.

The emerging sun carried light into the bedroom. Wearing a towel, boxers, and mismatched socks, he decided that it would be warm today. Instead of one of the many flannels that his wife had bought for him, he picked out a short-sleeved shirt. She would've already been outside and checked the sky.

"You can tell everything by el color del cielo," she'd said on many mornings. "Yes, it's hot now, viejo, but those clouds—the fat purple ones . . . you see them?—are bringing bad weather. Trust me."

"Oh, mujer, if you know so much, why was the laundry outside the last time it rained?"

"Forget it."

He glanced out the window for any so-called signs. Heavy winds weren't uncommon for this time of year in the desert, he guessed, so he grabbed a windbreaker. Five weeks after his wife's death, he was learning to make simple decisions like this alone.

After putting on his jeans, he went to the bedroom closet. In the far back, beyond his smelly shoes and the pregnant hamper, he pulled out the lunch bag. He was tempted to count the money, although he was the only one—except his wife—who knew about the altar. While he felt lucky to have found money, he wished that he had ten times more, figuring that was how much he needed to pay the bills piled on the dresser.

While the money hadn't freed him of his debts, it had made

day-to-day life less of a struggle for him. Just last week, he'd read a letter from Pima's school nurse without his heart running a marathon. After a quick trip to the Zaragoza Eye Clinic, his younger daughter now wore new reading glasses. Tony was glad no one— not his daughters, not the receptionist—had asked where he got the cash.

Like reading the tabloids, his trips into the closet were also a momentary escape. On the day that he discovered the secrets of Dolores's altar, he'd hurried home and searched the bedroom. As he dug through pockets, more than once the lavender smell of his wife's dresses and sweaters caused him to pause and take deep breaths. He'd bought her the same talc and perfume basket at Kress every Christmas since they'd been married. Although his search came up empty, except for balls of tissue and a pink rosary, he sensed that there was more hidden.

While dismantling the altar wasn't hard after he dropped El Santo Niño—even a little bit fun, he confessed to himself—he didn't feel good about searching his wife's dresser drawer. Inside, he discovered her undergarments. When he slipped a hand in the bundle of panties, the soft material stroked his calloused fingers. Digging further, he felt his heartbeat quicken when he came across his wife's bras, black and cream-colored. They smelled cleaner than anything he'd ever worn.

Moments like this, when he desired his wife, he returned to the drawer. He imagined her neck and shoulders as part of the silky contents. About to press his lips on a pair of panties, he heard the bedroom door open.

"Papi, we're up." Ramona and Pima stepped into the bedroom.

"Oh, hi"—he bumped into the dresser—"mijitas."

"What are you doing?" Ramona asked as she and her hermanita went over to the unmade bed.

"Uh . . . nothing." Tony hadn't moved. Now he pushed in the dresser drawer with his back. "Looking for a key."

"Which one?" Ramona asked.

"For the shop's office." He made a fist around the panties and shoved them in his pocket. "Are you ready?"

"Yes," Pima said at the same time Ramona said, "no."

"Well, what are you waiting for?" He went over and gave each one a kiss on the head. "C'mon, quit wasting sun."

When they left the room, he pulled the panties out of his pocket, closed his eyes, and inhaled with an open mouth. He returned them to the drawer with the rest of his wife's undergarments and made sure to shut the bedroom door on his way out.

Through the kitchen, he went to the front of the house and opened the curtains. Dust from the surrounding desert was an unwelcome guest in the Amoroza home. He'd have to remind the girls to keep la sala especially clean. The room had been their mamá's favorite. She'd said that while their family had little to offer, if they should ever have visita, at least they would be able to sit on comfortable furniture and feel welcomed. As it was after her funeral service, when mourners filled their home and brought armfuls of food and condolences.

A black-and-white photo of his wife rested on a corner table. She's wearing a polka-dot dress and crouching by a rosebush, her hair in a long braid and her lips parted as if she's about to laugh. A mirror above the photo was draped in black cloth, like his wife's church comadres had done to the other mirrors in the house.

He picked up the photo and kissed the frame's cold glass. "Ay, Dulcita, I wish you were here." He made sure that the candle next to the photo remained lit and brushed away a cobweb stretching from the wall to a vase of roses. "I'm no good without you." Instead of replacing them with fresh flowers, he'd leave these for the required period of Luto. He knew from his mother's death what was expected of him during the months of mourning.

In addition to covering the mirrors, his wife's church comadres had reminded him to store away the TV and record player. He didn't like all these nosy neighborhood women telling him what to do, but he'd decided to do as they said to avoid any chisme.

God knew how much they gossiped over coffee and menudo after Mass. The record player was broken anyway, but he did miss watching the midget wrestlers that always made him and his wife laugh.

One thing he hadn't been able to do since his wife's death was come up with the right words to give Pima the bad news. Her first piñata party, which had already been postponed, would have to wait, at least, until her next birthday. The papier-mâché Mama Smurf that he'd been out buying when his wife suffered her attack was stored away. The last time he went out to the shed, the piñata looked more like a balding elephant than a cartoon character. How do I explain the meaning of sacrifice? he wondered.

After his daughters slurped down bowls of cereal, they hurried to gather their things. He wasn't so hungry these days, so he went out and waited in the truck. It would take the girls at least ten minutes to come out, and that was about how much time it would take for his truck to warm up.

Although he shared an understanding with the decrepit Chevy, he still complained about the gears sticking as he made his way through the narrow, pothole-filled roads of their neighborhood. Most of the simple homes in Ysleta, including the Amorozas', were too small for the families that lived in them. Three or more generations of one family commonly lived under one roof.

Before Tony turned onto Zaragoza Road, he and the girls greeted their neighbors. Mr. Grijalva watering his lawn. La Señora Rivera pretending not to see her Pekinese shit in a neighbor's flower bed. Mr. and Mrs. Valdez enjoying their cafecitos on the porch. At one time, Tony had taken for granted that he and his wife would also enjoy similar mornings together. He quickly squinted the nostalgia to the corner of his eyes.

Driving to Mount Carmel Cemetery, he passed the graffiti-covered walls of the Kennedys, one of several housing projects in the Lower Valley. While he had survived a childhood on the Border, now as a single parent he worried a great deal about his daughters' well-being.

Every time they went outside, he told them to stay away from the park where cholos clutching paper bags loitered. At night, when he heard sirens and, more than once, gunshots, he was thankful that his daughters were tucked away in bed. Home was the safest place possible. At least that's what he repeatedly told himself as he tried to sleep in a half-empty bed.

He'd told his wife, as her life faded away in the hospital, that no matter how many hours he had to devote to the tire shop her daughters would grow up safely. They would one day move, like they'd always hoped, to another neighborhood. The girls would not be numbed by manual labor, he promised.

His wife passed away soon after, as if she'd been waiting for his guarantee of her daughters' future. From the moment he'd let go of her hand in the hospital to setting down her casket at the cemetery, he felt her strength slipping away. Without her, he was scared, and uncertain that he should have promised anything.

At a stoplight, where he had the truck in neutral and his foot on the gas, he tried to keep up with what his girls were going on about. They always talked over each other, especially when they were excited. From what he understood, it seemed that they had spent the last week at a party, not at school. They talked about boys, one who smiled at Ramona and said how pretty she looked. Pima swore she wasn't lying and crossed herself to prove it. Ramona blushed when he winked at her.

On many occasions, before and after his wife's funeral, his heart nearly emptied when they came home and cried for their mamá. As much as he worked to keep them safe in their home, when they were out in the community, they were reminded of their loss. The girls had told him how their teachers spoke to them in real soft voices. And how their school friends asked so many questions. How's the hospital? Is the funeral home a sad place? Does your father know how to cook?

After he willed the truck through the intersection of Alameda Avenue and Zaragoza Road, there was a pause in the girls' conversation. As if on cue, the truck gave out. It didn't sputter or jerk like so many other times before, it just conked out. He had enough sense to pop it into neutral, let it coast, and steer it to a vacant lot along Zaragoza Road. A car behind him honked. As much as he wanted to cuss at the driver, he didn't have the energy. When the truck came to a complete stop, he dropped his head on the steering wheel.

There was a long period of silence.

"Papi, are you okay?" Ramona put her hand on his shoulder. "What's wrong?"

"Todo," he mumbled.

He got out of the truck and slammed the door. When he raised the hood, the smell of gas shot through his nostrils and filled his head and empty stomach with fumes. He stepped away from the truck and fought the urge to vomit.

He leaned his head back and took several short breaths. Ramona got out of the truck and came to his side. Pima remained in the truck.

"Are you okay?" Ramona asked again.

He nodded.

There were few clouds in the sky. Sunday traffic was light in Ysleta. The bells of the Mission rang the hour. The cemetery was only a few blocks away.

He went over to the truck and slammed down the hood. "How about something to drink?" he said. "¿Unas aguas? Vamos a Juanita's."

"Let's go," Ramona said without hesitation.

"I have quarters." Pima was hanging out the window listening. She pulled out her change purse.

Tony and Ramona laughed. They knew that Pima had everything but quarters. Probably just some pennies and centavos she'd found around the house. Ever since she was old enough to count, she called loose change—whether it was Mexican money or the Susan B. Anthony coins Tony gave her—"quarters."

Juanita's was a home-turned-tiendita halfway between Amoroza Tires and Mount Carmel Cemetery. The small store was one of a few still left in Ysleta that did a decent business in the face of the flashy convenience stores. As long as anyone knew, it had been owned by Doña Juana, a Mexican woman who, rumor had it, fought alongside Emiliano Zapata. Tony told his daughters this every time they entered Juanita's as he pointed to a photo in the entryway. The crucifix next to the grainy images of Mexican solderas on horseback made it hard to call him a liar.

Señor Zubía, the man behind the store's counter, served Pima a snow cone, rainbow flavored: blue coconut, red strawberry, yellow pineapple, and green lime. Tony and Ramona ordered aguas de melón from a large container, where chunks of cantaloupe and ice floated in the orange water. Señor Zubía also gave Pima a cookie from the open box he kept behind the counter. She went to the back of the store where the toys were.

When Señor Zubía grinned, his decayed teeth gave away his weakness for sweets. On past trips to Juanita's, Tony and his wife had witnessed Doña Juana come into the store from the back room and yell at the old man for either reaching into the jars of loose candy or taking a box of cookies.

"How are we supposed to make any money, viejo, if you keep eating all the galletas?" Doña Juana had barked at Señor Zubía like he was a mischievous child. She scolded him for making her leave her TV game show and miss seeing someone win prizes by guessing whether there was a motorcycle, a VCR, or bags of dog food behind curtain #1, #2, or #3. The pobre viejito pretended not to hear the woman yelling.

Tony speculated about their relationship. They acted like a married couple, he'd told his wife, but as much as anyone in Ysleta knew—and the pair was a frequent subject of chisme among his wife's church comadres—they'd never married after meeting at the Bronco Bingo Parlor. At least not in a church. Maybe on the other side of the Border.

From witnessing the passion of the old couple's arguments,

Tony felt that they had what it took to keep each other interested. "What does it matter if they aren't married and simply share the same bed?" he'd told his wife. She disagreed, preaching to him that it was wrong, no matter how old they were, to live under the same roof without God's blessing.

"How's the shop?" Señor Zubía asked, spitting cookie crumbs.

"Not bad. Todavía viene mucha gente," Tony answered as he leafed through the magazines that Doña Juana kept in her tiendita. The magazines were mostly in Spanish and about telenovelas and fashion. He found the women on the covers attractive and quickly turned the pages, wondering if these women wore the same undergarments that his wife did. Lavender panties, black bras, washed nylons. Each night, he checked on two things: that the bag with the money was still in the closet and that the dresser drawer smelled like roses. He made a mental note to check how much talc and perfume was left among his wife's things.

"Have you taken any flowers to your mamá?" the old man, who was now hard to see seated behind the counter, asked Ramona.

She'd been reading a teen magazine and said nothing. Appearing surprised at the question, she turned to Tony, who also said nothing.

"No." Ramona put down the magazine and sipped on her agua de melón. "We haven't been. Maybe for Mother's Day."

Tony nodded, acknowledging his daughter's good idea to postpone their visit to the cemetery.

"We all miss Dolores. Mucho. She was . . . usted sabe—una mujer con tanta vida. Que Nuestro Dios la—"

"Señor Zubía, where's Doña Juana?" Ramona interrupted.

"En el otro lado." He pointed to the Zaragoza Bridge that was less than a mile away. "With her sons."

"Why didn't you go?"

"El puente's always a mess. Sudo mucho." He wiped his brow, as if just thinking about the hot hours waiting to cross over made him sweat.

"¿Como 'sta, Irene?" Ramona then asked the old man.

He threw his arms in the air and smacked his lips. "Quién sabe." Irene, his grandchild, had apparently not visited in some time. "Juanita says she only comes when she needs money. And to tell her 'No, get a job or go back to school.'" Señor Zubia paused as he repositioned a small fan behind the register. "¿Qué puedo hacer? She's my only nieta."

Tony wasn't surprised to hear of an absent Irene. One night at the dinner table, his daughter had told him that her friend was living with some cholo from Los Kennedys and was probably going to get in trouble. He took that to mean getting pregnant.

That night alone in bed, he stayed up worrying that he wouldn't be able to advise his daughters on such matters as dating, marriage, and least of all, sex. He imagined these awkward moments as a single father—first with Ramona, then with Pima—adding up like the past due notices that came in the mail. He wondered what it would have been like if his children had been boys. He was almost certain that they'd have been less of a worry. They would be able to take care of themselves, like he had from the time he left home at twelve until he married.

His thoughts consumed him. He didn't hear what else Ramona and Señor Zubia said about Irene. His presence returned to the store when Ramona went over to Señor Zubia and put an arm around the viejito. "I'll tell Irene to come visit. It's that sometimes she forgets." She kissed him on the cheek. "Even with me. I have to remind her that if we're gonna still be friends, then I can't be the only one trying."

The old man smiled at Tony and said, "I wish this one was my nietecita." He rubbed his eyes. "You're blessed, hombre. Two good daughters."

"I know I'm—" Tony's words were interrupted by a loud noise from the back of the store.

Pima was searching through a cardboard box and dropped something on the floor. The box was full of mostly junk, but occasionally customers could find something worth the price scrawled on the side: EVERYTHING. ONLY 75¢. SURPRISES. NO REFUNDS.

She continued to toss out many items: egg-shaped containers of pantyhose, plastic hairbrushes, cans of tuna, Oriental fans, dolls missing limbs, a wrestling mask, candy canes. She settled on a jigsaw puzzle.

She rushed over, her lips blue and her tongue red from the snow cone: "Papi, can I buy this?" She held up a box that was taped closed. "Please, papi, please, papi." The picture on the box was of a brilliant sunset over a mountain range and a blue river.

"Only if you use your quarters." He turned to Ramona and Señor Zubía. They laughed as Pima dumped the coins of her change purse on the counter.

He figured that the puzzle, especially if it was missing pieces, would keep Pima busy. And out of Ramona's way. From his bedroom, he often heard her telling her younger sister that she was too busy to play. Even if the recycled puzzle was a temporary solution, he felt he was doing the best he could.

As they left the store, Señor Zubía said good-bye through a mouthful of cookies.

"Adiós, saludanos a Doña Juana." Tony chuckled at how much the pobre viejo loved his sweets.

Outside the store, Tony put his hand out, expecting Pima to take it. He was surprised when Ramona slipped her hand in his. She snatched her sister's hand, and the three of them walked back to rescue the truck.

>>> <<<

After making up classes during the first part of the summer, Tony's daughters now spent what was left of their vacation at the tire shop. The city bus dropped them off in front of the Zaragoza Bakery. Mrs. Peña often waved them in and served them some sweet bread and horchata. Ramona had told him that his wife's close friend always asked them how things were at home. As with his wife's church comadres, he wasn't sure if he should appreciate Mrs. Peña's concern or resent it.

On this afternoon, he was happy for the pan de huevo she sent over. He took a big bite and peered out to the tire yard, where the girls were playing in the shadows cast by the mountains of tires. His daughters were trying to get the dog to play with them.

Soon after giving the stray entrance into his yard, he lost hope of it being anything other than a playmate for the girls. The caca-colored mutt—which looked nothing like the breeds he had imagined, not even after he bathed it—spent its days slumbering in any shade it could find. Under the truck. Next to a pile of tires. At least until it was time to eat. The dog enjoyed tipping over the hubcap that served as a bowl and eating its food covered in dirt. Stupid acts like this assured Tony that he'd chosen the right name, "Baboso," for the dog. The girls preferred to call it "Ojito." Of all things, it was missing an eye. And from the cloudiness of the one eye that it had, Tony wasn't so sure that the dumb animal could see at all.

The girls teased Baboso-Ojito enough to get it off the ground. It barked after them and tried to bite the blue jump rope that they dragged throughout the tire yard. When they saw their father at the window and yelled for him to come out and play, he listlessly shook his head and pointed to the tire shop. If he had spoken, the words would've been too familiar to his daughters: "There's too much work."

He washed down the last of his pan de huevo with a Fresca from the laundromat next door. Ramona had already finished doing many loads that were now drying. When he sent Pima to help her older sister, she came back and said Ramona didn't want any help.

He thought it best if Ramona kept busy. She seemed more relaxed when she had things to do. Helping Pima with her homework, cooking for the three of them, cleaning the house, even checking his math of the tire shop's receipts.

By mid-afternoon, under the preying sun, the day's arduous pace almost forced him to his knees. At least then, he considered, he would beg for an end. The last time he complained of chest pains, Dr. Muñoz had told him that he was having "ataques," as he claimed, but that they weren't "heart attacks."

"Panic attacks, Mr. Amoroza. Normal in times of stress." The doctor seemed so certain of his diagnosis.

"I'm not in panic," he'd told the doctor. He even turned to the nurse in the examination room and said, "Es mi corazón."

She didn't say anything. He took her forced smile as an insult.

At home, Ramona insisted on knowing what the doctor had said. He'd told her not to worry.

"What can I do? Let me help."

His daughter's words reminded him of his wife's before she took over managing the tire shop.

"You do too much already. 'stan locos," he said, knowing what a poor job he was doing of reassuring his daughter. "They just want money. All I need is some of your albóndigas, and I'll be okay."

While he intended to leave before it got dark today, he still had several tires to fix, not to mention running down to Western Auto for some adhesive, rubber plugs, and WD-40.

He knew the girls would be disappointed since he'd finally agreed to take them to the Lomaland Drive-In. The movie was one that all their friends had seen. While he'd only been to a few movies in his lifetime, he became interested when the girls said one of the movies playing at the drive-in was about a space alien. He wondered if this "E.T." looked like the ones in the *National Enquirer*.

Since they still weren't supposed to watch TV or listen to the radio, he felt a movie would be good for them. And it was unlikely that any of his wife's church comadres went to the drive-in. Over the last months, he, too, felt cheated. While their life as a family of three had started to glue itself together, their days were still clouded by Luto. Covered mirrors, dried flowers, burning candles.

All of it was becoming too much. He was certain that he was doing as poor a job as a mourner as he was as a father.

"We all make sacrifices we don't want to," he would again try to explain to the girls. Ramona would understand and say it was okay. Pima would simply slouch her shoulders and not say anything. He would promise they would go to the drive-in some other day.

The sun's descent into the Juárez Mountains signaled it was getting late. He was struggling with a new-model Chevy's lug nuts when Ramona stepped out of the tire shop. His face clenched, he grunted and didn't hear what she said. He dropped the tire iron and kicked the car, cursing, "Pinche llanta cabrona." Good thing for him that the driver was next door at the bakery. She'd raced in and said she was late for a party.

"Damn it, come off," he demanded of the lug nuts.

"Papi, oiga, papi, did you let Pima go out?" His daughter glanced from the tire yard to the desert to the car wash stalls.

"¿Qué? Goddamn tire," he said and held his back.

"Pima? Where is she?" Ramona repeated as she came out of the tire shop and stood by his side.

"I don't know. She was playing—I didn't let her—"

It was getting dark and neither of them had seen Pima for a couple of hours. Ramona had been going back and forth to finish the laundry while he tended to customers.

"You go see if she's at the Deluxx. I'll check the yard."

He trudged through the mesquite and yucca and creosote bushes clustered around the mounds of tires.

"Pima . . . Pima . . . are you back here?" he shouted in the tire yard. "Mija, where are you?"

He half-ran, half-walked to the far back of the tire yard, where he warned the girls not to go. His breathing grew heavy. His heart labored to keep up.

The desert behind his property was quiet. Nothing on the brown horizon. Although Baboso no longer had to dig his way into the yard, the holes under the chainlink fence remained. He'd neglected to cover them up. Fear clenched his chest after several minutes of no response. What if she crawled out? What if she's hurt?

His questions silenced when he didn't see any footprints other than his own. Sweat ran down his face as he hurried through the yard. He didn't know what he would find. The more he searched, kicking tumbleweeds and trash out of his way, peeking in and around the mountains of tires, the more vivid the dangers became.

Over the past months, he'd trained himself to expect the worst. If his wife could have an attack while he was out buying a piñata, then his daughter could easily fall in a hole while playing. Like that girl in Midland who was stuck for hours in a well. He'd heard about this incident first on the news and then read about it in the tabloids. A headline flashed into his mind: GIRL ABANDONED AMONG SNAKES AND JUNK.

What if she tripped into a patch of cacti? Or a rat bit her?

When he heard a dog bark, he rushed in that direction. "Baboso." His dry mouth failed in whistling. "Ven, perro."

As he rounded a high stack of tires, a fire ignited near his heart. Sharp pains shot down his body and paralyzed his lower half. Before he could brace himself, he tumbled into the tire stack. They pounded him like rocks. He managed to cover his head and avoid being hit in the face. His legs took most of the punishment. Each tire felt heavier than the previous one. Not until he was sure the last tire had fallen did he move his arm away from his face. He was buried up to his neck.

The fading sunlight and long shadows cast the desert even more desolate. Stillness consumed the tire yard.

Motionless for a long period, not knowing what else to do, he decided to try digging his way out. But he couldn't get his left arm up. It was jammed under the tires. He knew from a past accident that it was most likely broken. Dropping his head back, he felt soreness cage his body.

"Calmate, hombre. You'll be okay." He closed his eyes and tried to gather himself.

His heart beat inside his chest like his truck's worn pistons. His pills, which he'd forgotten to take after lunch, were in his pocket. He couldn't reach them. And when he tried to move a tire with his good arm, the pile shifted, pressing down harder on him. He gave up after little effort.

"Okay. If you want me now, go ahead. Estoy listo. Take me, take all this, it's yours.

"Do you hear me? No quiero más."

After a few deep breaths, he continued to shout, although he doubted anyone was listening.

"I'll go now, won't fight. You win.

"Ever since you left, I've worked to do as you wanted. I've done all I can. It's hard. I can't promise no more."

With his eyes still closed, he put his good arm inside his overalls. He clasped the scapular under his T-shirt. Although he'd forgotten what promise he made to his wife when she gave it to him, he put it on every morning along with clean underwear and clean socks.

He hoped the scapular would help him bargain his way out of this mess.

About to begin whatever Spanish prayers he remembered, he felt wetness. Wiping at his face, he opened his eyes and realized it was Baboso. The mutt was panting over him, splattering drool on his mouth and cheeks.

"Papi, papi, what happened?" Pima ran up behind Baboso. She held an empanada and had jelly and sugar all over her mouth. "Are you all right?"

He was glad to see her in one piece and said nothing for a moment. His heartbeat matched his irregular breathing.

"What should I do?" She leaned over him and tried to keep Baboso from licking her mouth.

When he registered a scared tone in her voice, he steadied his breathing and managed to say, "Go. Tell Ramona. Call for help. Go. Go, mijita."

Pima ran toward the tire shop. Baboso stayed with him. The mutt continued to slobber and lick at his face. When he stared into its rheumy pupil, a mini crystal ball, he knew the dog's vision was greater than he previously thought. He yelled at the mutt to cut it out—"Get the hell outta here, stupid dog"—but, really, he felt lucky to have some company.

What he felt most guilty about the day that his wife had her attack was that she'd been alone. She shouldn't have been working here at all, he thought. Much less alone. No one to help. He decided in the hospital's waiting room that when his moment came, above all, he didn't want to be alone.

Sweat stinging his eyes and blood rushing through his heart, he wasn't sure how long he'd been buried in the yard before he heard the sirens. And, as the familiar cries of the Ysleta Fire Department grew louder and louder, he became aware of a formation of clouds. They swept in fast from south of the Border.

Their swollen size shrouded what was left of the sunlight. A darkness many times as black as the mountains of tires spilled over everything.

The thick mass of clouds circled above him like a whirlpool. Sand and debris stirred in the air. Tumbleweeds and stray hubcaps darted across the tire yard as if looking for refuge. Baboso barked and jumped with the possessed spirit of a puppy with two good eyes.

The motion of el cielo—*sky and heaven*—hypnotized him.

"¿Qué 'sta pasando?" He clutched the scapular in his fist, closed his eyes, and leaned his head back. "No entiendo."

The dark made the wait of the next moments feel like hours.

When he felt a wet stream run down his body, he opened his eyes and expected it to be raining. No. The clouds hadn't sliced open.

It was Baboso. The mutt was pissing on him.

Rather than get mad, he was comforted that he wasn't the only one who was scared.

>>> <<<

Over the last month, Tony had convinced himself that he was too tired to work. He swore to his legs and feet that there was no way that they were going to step back into the tire shop, much less the tire yard. His right arm might as well have been in a cast too, since he promised himself that he would never again lift another tire, flat or otherwise, or grip a tire iron or wrench or screwdriver. For the first time in who knows how long, his hands weren't black with grease.

He surrendered to a daytime routine unlike his former one as a laborer. Opening his eyes around ten, dragging himself to the bathroom, getting back in bed, sleeping another two hours, reading his tabloids, eating the lunch Ramona left for him, cutting and pasting, taking a nap before dinner.

If he had to go to the kitchen, he ignored the living room and its symbols of Luto. He resented that he couldn't walk anywhere in his house, in fact, without being reminded of his past life as a married man. Only a year ago, he remembered, things were good. And getting better.

That was when his wife had convinced him about maybe buying a bigger house. With the steady business the tire shop was doing, they could at least afford to look around, she'd told him. He was reluctant. The tire shop was making money, but he hated the idea of applying for a loan, he'd told his wife. After many talks in bed—when she cuddled next to him and whispered that it wasn't for them but for the girls—he'd said that she was probably right. Once again, it was at his wife's request that he considered making a large investment. The first time was when she urged him to buy the tire shop when his boss retired.

The house that his wife had seen for sale in the paper was a short drive north on Zaragoza Road. Newer schools, a park nearby, not so many gangs, she'd told him. They drove by the address several times on their way back from the grocery store.

White stucco with blue trim, a yard with plenty of grass, and a Mexican elder and mulberry, lots of shade. There was also an arched entryway. And what his wife had liked best of all were the front doors. As they'd parked in front of the house, she'd told him she was sure that they were custom-made, possibly shipped from México, where she'd seen men labor over such beautiful wood.

The last time they'd checked to see if the house was still for sale, she convinced him to pretend that he was lost and go see if she was right—that the doors were handcrafted. He was nervous the whole time he walked up the pathway through the well-cared-for lawn.

He paused when he reached the doors, put his hands on the wood—his flesh the same rich color—and ran his fingers over the smooth curves and sharp edges. For a minute, he forgot that this wasn't his home. When he noticed the windows on each side of the doors, he realized that someone might see him standing outside. He didn't want them to call the police, so he knocked, reminding himself that he was supposed to be lost.

When no one answered, he felt relieved and disappointed. He turned to his wife, who had half her body hanging out of the truck's passenger-side window. He dried his palms on his pant legs and rang the doorbell. He had come this far, he had to know who lived here. How many children? What color are the rooms? Where do you have the TV? After the third ring of the bell, he reasoned no one was home.

In the truck, when his wife asked him what he was doing there so long, he said, "I wanted to look into the eyes of the people who own this house, those doors."

"What would you have said?" she asked.

"I'm not sure."

Stretched out on his wife's side of the bed, he fought off the foolish memories of what should have been by dragging himself to the bathroom. He couldn't remember how many days had passed since he last showered. If it were up to him, he wouldn't care about such things. Ramona protested. When he told her that he didn't want to get his cast wet, she brought him a plastic bag and some tape. When he asked for the hospital bedpan, she said she'd put it outside for Ojito's food. The dog had been brought over from the tire shop.

Last night, when he insisted he wasn't hungry, his daughter told him that enough time had passed for him to begin healing.

"It's not good for you to stay in bed all the time," she said while she changed his sheets. "The doctors said you can even lift things, if you want."

"I know you want to be a nurse, but what makes you think you're a doctor?" he thought to say but didn't.

While he hadn't fully accepted his wife's death, he understood how Ramona was so unlike him. She didn't seem aware of everything falling apart around them. And if she was, she wasn't scared. She had taken the death of her mother as a challenge, it seemed. This impressed him.

After showering, keeping the left side of his body dry, he shaved and put on some clean pajama bottoms and a T-shirt. He made the bed before he propped up a pillow and got to work. Ramona, who was now working part-time at the Zaragoza Bakery, brought him a stack of tabloids every week. Having read them all more than once, he took out the scissors and tape from Pima's school box. His latest collage on the bedroom wall was almost complete.

Since the incident in the tire yard—*heaven and sky*—he'd been paying more attention to reports of natural phenomena across the world.

PREDICTED SNOWSTORM HITS MIDDLE OF SAHARA

TSUNAMI SEASON LINKED TO BIRTH OF TRIPLETS

ITALIAN BLACKSMITH CALLS WHITE TREE A SIGN

He was positive that his own vision in the tire yard was as dramatic as any of these stories. If he could only find the words, the exact descriptions, he would attempt to gather his story. Getting someone else to write his experience and selling the story was one of his ideas to make money. While he had many ideas locked away in his head, he hadn't acted on any of them. Dolores's altar money was gone, and with the tire shop closed again, his bank account was shrinking like a tire with a steady leak.

His story, like many in the tabloids, had only one witness: Antonio Amoroza, widower, father of two, laborer, from Ysleta, Texas.

By the way Baboso carried on, the mutt didn't seem affected one way or another by the experience. When Tony had asked the girls if they'd seen anything unusual in the sky that day, they shook their heads and appeared even more concerned. He remembered hearing the paramedics who showed up on the scene ask his daughters if he was on medication. If he hadn't had the oxygen mask over his mouth, he would've told the paramedics and his daughters that he wasn't imagining things. Pills or no pills. He knew what he saw. Nobody could take that from him.

Now, weeks later, outside of the tire yard, while he wasn't so clear of the details of what he'd seen, whatever it was, he knew the experience had changed him. While his limbs and organs remained vulnerable, his mind was in fine working condition.

Days of rest had helped clear his head. He made patched-together decisions. For him. For his daughters. And ultimately for the future of this family. He prayed that these decisions were enough.

For the moment, there was one last thing to do. He pushed himself up from the bed, walked over to the nightstand, and found a sheet of paper. With a blue marker, he scrawled out a sentence that had been taking shape in his mind, but had been, until now, out of his reach.

MOURNING SKY: HEAVEN APPEARS TO TIRE MAN

He taped his words on the wall next to the others.

"There, finally," he told himself. "Now I don't have to look at that crack anymore."

Noticing the fading light in the room, he guessed it was a few minutes before the girls would be coming home. After he put on some jeans and sneakers, he began to clean up the bedroom. He threw the piles of wadded tissues, empty soda cans, and cut-up tabloids in the trash. The bottles of medication went into a dresser drawer. At the same time, he took the pile of bills out from under San José's head and shoved it into the drawer.

He said to his wife's loyal saint in Spanish, "Why worry so much when I have so much." He kissed the top of the saint's head and placed it next to his scapular and Dolores's pink rosary on the dresser—the beginnings of an altar.

He carried all the plates, glasses, and utensils from his room to the kitchen, clutched between his cast and his chest, piled them next to the girls' breakfast dishes, and filled the sink with soap and water. In the pantry he found plastic wrap and covered his cast. He was washing the dishes when the girls came home.

"Papi, what are you doing?" Ramona asked as she set some grocery bags on the table.

"What, you've never seen me work?" He blew suds off his plastic-covered arm.

"No, it's just that—"

"What's in the bags?"

"Oh, I thought I would make flautas tonight. And some calabacitas."

"Sounds good. I'm hungry." He continued to rinse the dishes while his daughter put away the groceries.

"Where's Pima?"

"She went to bother Ojito. I'll tell her to come help you."

"No, no. Let her play."

The smell of onion and garlic filled the kitchen by the time he finished the dishes. Ramona was slicing squash when he snatched a handful of grated cheese from a plate. She playfully slapped his hand. He responded by kissing her cheek. She appeared surprised by his affection.

"Hey, mijita," he said as he walked out of the kitchen into the backyard. Pima was rolling around on the ground with the dog.

"What's wrong, papi?" Pima jumped to her feet, came over to Tony, and pointed to his cast.

"Nothing." He raised his arms like Popeye.

"Did you hurt your arm again?"

"No, I was washing," he said. "Here, pull." He let her take hold of the plastic wrap as he turned his arm. She rolled it up into a ball. They threw it back and forth until it fell and the dog scooped it up. As his daughter chased after the mutt, he felt some satisfaction from having the dog enter their lives. He didn't care if it continued to dig up the yard, and he'd even started calling it Ojito.

He walked over to the cuartito in the backyard. The wooden shed was a miniature junkyard. Manual lawn mower. Open bags of cement. Busted bicycles. More tires. More rims. A crib. A cracked sink. What he was looking for was hanging from a nail. He stood on a paint can and took it down. He brushed off whatever cobwebs and dust he could before carrying it out of the shed.

Pima yelled when she saw the weathered piñata. "Lookit—Mama Smurf!" A few pieces of blue crepe paper clung to the hardened pieces of newspaper. The print and photos were faded, no headlines legible. Mama Smurf was missing an eye, and her stomach was bent. He was surprised that his daughter recognized the cartoon character.

"Do you remember?"

"My birthday."

"Well, today, it's all of our birthdays."

"Papi, what do you mean?"

"C'mon, let's eat first." The piñata left a trail of paper as he and Pima carried it inside.

He was sure the Mexican candy in the piñata was spoiled, but it didn't matter now. All that was important was that he'd decided his family would celebrate.

While Ramona put out a cucumber and tomato salad and a pitcher of fresh lemonade, he led Pima through the living room. In his hand he clutched the black-and-white photo of his wife. He assured Pima that it was all right to blow out the candle and remove the vase of dried flowers.

"Is Luto over, papi?"

"Yes, mijita, it is for us," he said as he pulled the black cloth away from the mirror.

"Are you sure?" Ramona stood in the doorway to the living room. "It's only a few more months."

"Come on."

He led the two of them to the hall closet. Along the way, he told Ramona to uncover the mirror in the entryway. He smiled at his daughter's reflection. After putting his wife's picture in a shoebox with the candle and flowers, he put the box in the closet. They made room for it by taking out the TV.

Pima cheered as if she was opening birthday presents.

They carried the TV to the kitchen and set it on the counter. It took a while to warm up, and the color picture needed to be focused. Pima turned the knob until she found a cartoon on a Spanish station.

When Ramona saw the piñata propped up in her usual chair, she sat across from her father. The three of them ate flautas with guacamole between bursts of laughter. When the Roadrunner said, "Beep-beep," Tony also said, "Beep-beep." Soon, all three of them answered, "Beep-beep. Beep-beep. Beep-beep."

"Mija, this is delicious. How'd you get to be such a good cook?" Tony said to Ramona as he wiped his mouth.

"From mamá." Ramona kept her eyes on her plate.

Pima turned away from the TV to watch for Tony's reaction. He knew that she, especially, would always look to him for assurance.

After a short period of silence, he said, "I know, we all learned something good from her."

Pima nodded, although there hadn't been any question. She took a big bite of her flautas, pushed her plate back, and jumped out of her seat. "C'mon. Piñata time." She hugged Mama Smurf, denting it even more, not caring if she got full of dirty cobwebs.

He and Ramona followed Pima to the backyard. They got a rope from the cuartito, tied it between branches, and hung the piñata. It swayed like a misshapen bell. Ojito barked and jumped at the fellow one-eyed creature. Tony fetched a wooden handle from a busted shovel in the cuartito.

"Who goes first?" Pima jumped around anxiously.

"Do you want to?" A smile ran across Tony's face.

"Yes. Yes."

He offered the makeshift bat to her. Before she could take it, Ramona spoke. "No, let papi go. He should hit it first."

He knew that Pima would be disappointed, yet he was anxious to take the first swings. His palms grew moist. His heart beat strong.

His feet parallel to his shoulders, one in front of the other, he squatted, and tucked in his arms. Even with one arm in a cast, he knew he could break it open.

Before he took his turn, he glanced at his daughters—a brilliance buried in their eyes. Hope and expectation.

As if finally fulfilling a promise, he swallowed a deep breath and swung with all his heart.

>>> *Río Bravo* <<<
(a corrida)

With one headlight guiding his way, Chuco drove down a pot-hole-filled road, not paying attention in what direction he was going. He was mad at his girlfriend, Xochitl—actually at her father, who'd come home drunk again. Since she was the only daughter in the family, she was obligated to stay home and make sure her pobre papá didn't hurt himself. She had three brothers, but they were always out getting into some kind of trouble, she'd told Chuco. One night, after many hours of drinking, her father had come home and nearly burned down the house while cooking some frijoles con chorizo. Gracias a Dios for a neighbor. She was coming over to sell Xochitl some cosmetics when she saw smoke coming out of the kitchen. If not for the neighbor, the house would've been nothing but ashes when Xochitl came home from a date.

On this Friday night, when Chuco went over after work with two bottles of the sweet wine that Xochitl liked and their favorite spot in the desert waiting, she was bound to her home. He had wanted to tell her that she was dumb for caring for her father like a child. If the son of a bitch hadn't been passed out on the sofa, sucking a beer bottle like a pacifier, Chuco might've kicked his ass. Este pinche hombre, even if he is her papá, doesn't deserve her, Chuco thought. He deserves no one.

Fueled by anger, Chuco had left Xochitl's and crossed over into the rest of the night.

He parked his beat-up truck in a corner off an unpaved road, making a mental note of the location. A weathered mural of Villa's Revolucionarios was on the wall across from where he stood. Once, Chuco and his carnal had gotten drunk and forgotten where they'd parked. It took them hours into the next morning to sober up and remember. By that time, someone had broken into the truck and taken the stereo and some tools.

Although Chuco had already finished the bottles of wine, he wasn't a heavy drinker anymore like when he ran around with Los Vampiros, his old ganga. But without Xochitl, who didn't like him to drink so much that he reminded her of her pobre papá, he was more likely to spend all of his paycheck.

It would still be an hour or so before the regular Friday night crowd would filter into the Río Bravo. Other than Chuco, only two men sat at the bar counter, and there were a few people in the back. It was hotter in the bar than outside. When Chuco asked the bartender if he could turn the fan closest to him on, the cabrón gave him a blank stare and continued drying some mugs, prompting Chuco to take off his flannel shirt. He didn't care if the undershirt he had on was stained with oil and dirt from his jale. The bartender did seem to take notice of the tattoos on Chuco's arm—blood dripping off fangs and VLV in Old English script.

Other than a variety of beer advertisements displaying bikini-clad models and boasting of their products—LA MAS FINA, BEER WITHOUT BORDERS, WILD RIVER THIRST—Río Bravo's brick walls were bare. A tarnished marker posted outside read that Río Bravo dated back before the turn of the century and even claimed many celebrities and heroes as patrons.

After sitting at the bar counter a long while, Chuco turned his attention to the back area, where there was a jukebox spinning 45's, an empty dance floor, and a pool table. A man and two women were shooting a game. The man was the tallest in the bar, and his stomach was a wide, taut drum that proudly hung over his silver belt buckle in the shape of Tejas. He also showed off an expensive western hat and snakeskin boots. He reminded Chuco of some cowboy he'd seen in a late-night TV movie.

Chuco finished his third glass of whiskey from a bottle off the top shelf. He placed a wad of bills on the counter and ordered a beer. A friendly buzz kicked around in his head as his thoughts turned to the "TV Caballero" and how lucky he was to have two women in his company tonight.

While the younger of the two took her turn at the pool table, the other one, who appeared to be much older, went over to the jukebox. A fast corrida came on. Chuco recognized it as the latest single by Xochitl's favorite group. The TV Caballero's older companion was squeezed into a see-through blouse, red spandex shorts, and high heels, also red. Given her large size, she kept up well with the guitars and trumpets of the corrida, carelessly dancing around the pool table, thrusting her wide hips to both sides. The pool table rocked on its poor legs when she bumped into it.

After another corrida, a ranchera came on. Chuco recognized it from his mamá's record collection. Winded from all her dancing, the big woman dropped herself on the TV Caballero's lap, chugging down the rest of his bottle. Belting out a mariachi yell, the man lassoed the woman with his arms, his left hand clutching the inside of her thigh. Chuco watched as she laughed wildly at something the TV Caballero whispered. She gave him a slobbery kiss. Her nipples peeked out through her blouse.

Chuco wondered into the bottom of his whiskey glass if the women were the man's lovers. Or putas who did a good business in Río Bravo, mostly with anxious GI's from the army base.

Thinking that the older woman sitting on the TV Caballero's lap was one of the whores in the bar, Chuco felt differently toward the other woman. Without all her makeup, he wouldn't have guessed her to be older than sixteen, Xochitl's age. Her hair was cut short like a boy's, and he liked the way it bared her face. A tiny nose rested between eyes the color of the eight ball, and the mole on her cheek accented her ripe lips.

In a suede miniskirt and a halter top, this younger woman paraded around the pool table. She bent over with her backside toward Chuco at the bar counter and wiggled with the rhythm of the cumbia now playing, one of his favorites whenever he was on the dance floor. His mind was saturated with the best the bar had for customers with open wallets. He leered at the young woman. Wet grins sprouted across the faces of the men sitting next to him.

A longing drew Chuco closer to the young woman. Near the pool table, he bought a pack of cigarettes from one of the many vendors in the bar. He fixed his eyes on the young woman, from her sandals to her thighs, his wants leading his thoughts to the blossomed warmth under her miniskirt. She sank a striped ball in the corner pocket.

When she caught him staring, she motioned for him to come over. Not trusting his luck, he hesitated before taking a step. She asked him in Spanish for a cigarette. He handed her the one he'd just raised to his lips. While the woman on the TV Caballero's lap was light-skinned, this young woman was as morena as the Tarahumaras begging outside.

He began chasing a fantasy of him and this woman. Later that night, them alone, away from the noise and stares of the bar. They kiss without knowing each other's names, her pushing her eager tongue into his mouth. She undresses for him, kneading his hands on her flesh, craving for him to touch her where it feels good. Her head falls back as he bites her nipples and sucks her breasts, the size of membrillos. Hungering to be inside, he lifts her from her waist, pulling her toward his ready—

"¿Qué miras, pendejo?" The large woman jumped off the TV Caballero's lap. "Le estoy hablando, cabrón. ¿No oyes?"

An unsuspecting Chuco gave the approaching older woman a surprised look. Her tone signaled danger. Like the scars on his torso, her words were reminders of past incidents. He carefully retreated to his waiting stool.

The woman continued yelling and cussing in Spanish from the rear of the barroom, asking him if he liked what he saw in her friend. If he did, she shouted, would he care to spend his money on some fun in the back room, possibly with both women? She said all this in a tone that was more of a challenge than an offer. He ignored her by having another beer, making a sour face when he sucked on a lime wedge.

Although the hostile woman had made her way across the now-full barroom and was only a few feet away from him, she kept hollering. The way she threw her flabby arms around boasted of her untamed reputation among Río Bravo's other patrons. Knowing better, most of them didn't turn to see what was going on. Chuco was surprised that he could hear her over the loud voices and rock song playing, probably put on by one of the GI's who'd since entered the bar.

Chuco hadn't realized from a distance how hefty and ugly this woman was. While the man reminded him of an obese gunfighter, this woman could be a female wrestler he'd seen at Lucha Libre— "La Giganta." She'd been one of the most notorious wrestlers featured on Sunday afternoons. La Giganta was famous for climbing on the ropes, blindfolding herself, and flopping on her already beaten opponents.

His drunken state left him partially unaware of the match brewing between him and this ready foe. On his stool, thinking that she would tire and go back to her two friends at the pool table, he felt lucky that the woman's TV-Caballero escort hadn't made a move. If there were to be a face-to-face fight, Chuco would rather hit an oversized woman and flee than get booted to death by a man who would also triumph at Lucha Libre.

The woman's verbal assault made it impossible for him to ignore her. Deciding that La Giganta was in the mood for some crazy trouble, he swallowed the rest of his beer and another shot of whiskey and put a large bill on the bar, signaling his intended exit to the bartender. He grabbed his flannel shirt and headed for the door, intent on making up with Xochitl.

"I'll tell her I'm sorry," he said to himself. "I'm sorry that—"

His mind went blank. The sharp blow on his poorly built frame was followed immediately by a second strike. Knocked to the ground, he caught a glimpse of La Giganta raising a cue stick high above her head and bringing it down on him again.

His vision turned red. He struggled to get an arm up in defense. When La Giganta brought the fat end of the cue stick down on him again and again and again, his arm went as limp as a wet noodle. He heard the muffled sound of people in the bar yelling-laughing-cheering as more blows descended upon him. The roar of a bullfight arena kicked around in his head in the long period when no one came to his aid. All the while, he resembled a broken marionette thrown lifeless on the floor.

Not until the bar's security guard—a pudgy man who didn't card anyone but the youngest-looking gringos—rushed in to see what all the noise was about did La Giganta stop using Chuco for a piñata.

Pulled off her bloody prey, La Giganta wiped rivers of slobber from around her mouth and warned Chuco to never look so eagerly at a woman without expecting to pay a price. Her young friend cowered by the pool table. La Giganta took the money that had fallen from Chuco's wallet and spat on him before she went back to her TV Caballero and her female friend. La Giganta kissed her full on the lips. The TV Caballero's fleshy face burned bright red. They were sure to celebrate La Giganta's victory well into the night.

The security guard and the bartender wrapped Chuco's flannel shirt around his bloody head like a turban and dragged him behind a velvet curtain. They dropped him facedown on a bare mattress on the floor. It reeked of sweat and semen.

Fighting to breathe, Chuco struggled to turn himself over. A light bulb swayed hypnotically on a wire hanging from the water-stained ceiling. His body tightened with soreness as roaches scampered along the plaster walls. His heart throbbed inside his chest like a heat-filled room ready to explode.

In his last moments of consciousness, he heard guitars-accordion-trumpets. The corrida was distorted by the sounds of a couple on a nearby mattress. A GI had his pants pulled down to his knees, his hairless, pale ass in the air. The half-dressed woman he was on top of had her witchlike fingernails, dipped in glittery purple, embedded in his freckled back. She moaned exaggerated words of encouragement: "Ay mi güerrriiitooo, qué suave eres. No pares, mi güerrriiitooo, no pares ..."

Chuco woke up not sure where he was or how long he'd been out. Dirty light soaked through a window. He thought he was dreaming when an illuminated figure stood over him. When his one eye that wasn't swollen shut focused, he realized that the angel-image was the younger woman from inside the barroom. Beneath her mask of makeup—traces of deep reds on her lips and thick blue-black lines around her eyes—she had to be younger than what he'd previously thought, possibly as young as thirteen.

With the buzz in his head now an enemy-of-a-headache, he listened as best he could to what she was saying. She explained in

Spanish that her friend, "La Giganta" to Chuco, was drunk and hadn't meant to hurt him. She was only looking out for her, defending her honor, she expressed while avoiding eye contact.

He heard what she said, but he still didn't completely understand what had happened hours earlier in the barroom or what would happen if he kissed this teenager-woman like he desired right now. Without too much thought, he stood as best he could, stroked the mole on her cheek, and parted her lips with his fingers. As he leaned in to kiss her, she drew back.

The nameless stranger took his hand and led him through the velvet curtain back into the Río Bravo. It was empty except for the security guard watching cartoons, a Tarahumara breast-feeding her baby in a corner, and two soldiers passed out beneath the bar. The young woman poured Chuco water from a plastic beer pitcher and disappeared out the front door. The water helped quench his thirst. He grabbed a chunk of ice out of his mug and rubbed his forehead where the brand of last night's beating was still raw.

He scanned the bar for any clues to what had happened and, most important, why he was still here. With the bar quiet and empty, it didn't seem anything like his beaten body remembered. He was bothered more by his longing for this young stranger than about having had his ass kicked by La Giganta. Though he was glad she wasn't around. He wasn't sure if anyone or anything was worth the risk of a second round with her.

The young woman brought back a torta and put it on the table. He unwrapped the wax paper as she went over by the door. Chewing the stringy meat and potatoes bathed in chile, he spied on the woman talking with the security guard, who was old enough to be her grandfather. The way she played around—her hands raking his chest hair—made him jealous. Chuco wasn't drunk anymore, so regaining some honor by challenging the security guard was out of the question.

He finished his torta and got up to leave. When the young

woman came over, he wanted to ask her her name, where she lived, and maybe if he could see her again, but the words—in either of his two languages—didn't escape his mouth. He simply thanked her for the water and torta and dug out the bills that he had left in his pockets. When he offered them, she appeared embarrassed. She glanced at the security guard, who had one eye on the TV, and she took the money and stuffed it in her bosom.

She and Chuco stared at each other, uncertain of what to do next. With no words said, she stood on her tiptoes, kissed him on the cheek, and went and sat on the security guard's lap. As Chuco approached the front door, out of the corner of his eye, he saw the man reach inside her blouse and grab more than just the money.

When Chuco stepped out of the Río Bravo, the sun hit him in the face like a policeman's flashlight. He walked down several blocks, crossed streets, and peered down alleys, searching for his truck. As he was about to give up, he spotted an army riding into battle across a wall of graffiti.

¡Viva Villa! ¡Viva Villa!

Other than starbursts of bird shit on his hood and front window, his truck was as he'd left it. Even the loose spare in the bed hadn't been disturbed. The truck had survived the night better than he had. Once again, he would make it back.

>>> ***Rio Grande*** <<<

KMART

One second we're picking up lunch at Chico's Tacos. The next, Steve's speeding through a red light, nearly taking out a Datsun.

I braced myself.

"What the hell are you doing?"

"Check it out, man."

"What?"

"There."

He screeched his van to a stop in the parking lot of a Kmart. One of who knows how many in El Paso.

Trays of rolled tacos in soupy salsa splattered all over the place.

Rivers of red cheese sauce ran down the dashboard onto my jeans and canvas high-tops.

Not sure what he was worked up about, I watched Steve bolt over to the side of the store. And like so many times before, I decided if it's good enough to incite my best friend, it must be worth seeing. I got out of the van and sloshed behind him.

About ten yards away, there was a crowd of blue shirts— Kmart employees, I figured—checking out la migra. One Border Patrol agent herded men and women and children into a bile-green Suburban while another rummaged through the illegals' belongings: limes, gum, candy, cigarettes, the usual stuff you see them selling in parking lots and at intersections around town.

Just when I thought that things were going very business-like, a man and a teenage girl slipped out of the Suburban and took off running. One of la migra, a gringo, went after the man, and the other agent, a Chicano, chased the girl. While the man was slow and an easy catch, the teenager was quick and darted in and out of the Dumpsters behind Kmart, scurrying like a scared rabbit in the desert.

I edged closer to the scene. The Chicano agent was closing in on the girl when he tripped. Before he got up, he yelled. The girl froze. I couldn't really see everything from where I was, but I bet he drew his gun.

The gringo agent had already locked away his man and saddled himself in the driver's seat by the time his partner led the girl back to the Suburban. The Chicano agent, who sized up like the welterweight Roberto Durán, jabbed the girl with his baton in our direction.

I was about to grab Steve, who was eyeing some blond Kmart babe, and put his ass in the van when the Chicano agent struck the girl. She screamed and swung a sack of limes that she hadn't let go of. Agent Durán got real angry. He smacked her again. Her limes spilled onto the ground. The Chicano agent stomped them as he kicked her with his black Tony Lamas. A wild dance.

The girl balled up on the asphalt and endured the Chicano agent's beating as the other illegals witnessed it from the caged Suburban. The girl was about to take the last blow before, I was sure, she was going to pass out when the gringo agent jumped out of the Suburban. He dashed to the scene, snatched his partner's baton, and knocked him to the ground. "That's enough. You crazy?"

Just like John Wayne in *True Grit,* the gringo agent sauntered over to the girl, who'd taken refuge under the Suburban. Tears cleaned streaks down her face. Her blouse was ripped of its buttons. Before he reached her, the Chicano agent rushed up behind him and jumped on his back, mounting his partner like a bronc. The next thing I knew, they were going at it.

MANOS DE PIEDRAS VS. THE DUKE. A helluva match.

A mass of green uniform rolled around in the oil stains and gravel of Kmart's parking lot. Arms and legs and boots flew into each other's bodies. If their Stetsons hadn't been knocked off, it would have been hard to tell exactly who was who. The Chicano had a brown bald spot. The other agent's hair burned gold in the Texas sun.

The illegals jailed in the Suburban rocked it back and forth, making all kinds of noise, presumably rooting for the gringo. A first, I'm sure.

While my body cramped watching the beating of the girl, I was exhilarated by the Border Patrol agents beating the hell out of each other. The bout excited me so much that when both men collapsed from exhaustion I wanted to jump in and start them fighting again.

I might've done something, who knows what, while the agents were at their weakest if I hadn't been distracted by the Mexican teenager. She crawled from under the Suburban over to some keys that had fallen out during the fight. When she noticed that I was watching her, she paused, for only a second—met my eyes with hers—and hurried to set her friends loose.

Like fans at a track meet, Steve and the rest of the crowd

cheered the illegals' exodus from the Suburban. The two Border Patrol agents remained on their backs—faces bloodied, chests heaving, uniforms drenched in sweat. They didn't move until ambulances arrived and carted each one away separately, the Suburban left behind like a robbed safe—an empty reminder of the day's losses.

Many members of la migra showed up on the scene. By the way one of them barked orders at other agents, I guessed he must've been the Border Patrol chief. I didn't say shit about anything, especially about the illegals; that would be included in some official report. They were long gone by then and had probably found another Kmart to resume their business.

RIO GRANDE

Hours later, Steve drove west on the levee road that ran along the Border Highway. A full moon hung over the Sierra de Juárez on the other side. Its dirty-orange reflection played in the full river that cut us off from the Third World, a whole other time zone.

I absorbed each bump in the levee road as if I was one of the van's shocks. Steve was doing his best to miss the holes. At least that's what he swore he was doing. A few times, a tire slipped off the narrow road, jolting me to notice that he was drunker than I thought. He kept insisting that our buddies were having a bonfire out here.

While I was used to his wild driving, especially on nights when we'd both had lots to drink, the earlier scene in the Kmart parking lot had left me nervous. A feeling had crawled under my skin. A chilling numbness, like when one of your limbs falls asleep. My whole body felt this way.

"Slow down, fucker." I snapped on my seat belt. "You're gonna put us in the river." I had to yell so he could hear me over Van Halen. We'd unbolted and removed the rear seats to make room for his latest score—four huge speakers.

"Don't worry, Joe, I got it under control." He flashed me his white-Chiclet smile.

"Just don't kill us."

"Ah, c'mon, would I do that?"

This is what I remember: He popped a cigarette in his mouth, pulled out a lighter, which dropped between his legs, the road there one second, gone the next, a sharp decline, gripping the dash, an approaching tree, yelling, and thud.

I might've also reached for the steering wheel when Steve took his eyes off the road and his hands off the wheel. All I know for sure is that we were lucky to have gone right not left, cottonwood not Rio.

It took all of "Best of Both Worlds"—Eddie Van Halen's guitar screeching like cicadas in the night—for my head to stop somersaulting and realize we'd crashed. The van was kissed up against one of the many trees next to the levee road.

My door was jammed, so I escaped through the side window. When I landed outside, I spotted Steve teetering in front of the van. I might've told him I was okay and asked how he was if he hadn't seemed more concerned about taking a piss. Head leaned back, he stared at a starless sky. A river of piss flowed with the fluorescent antifreeze gushing out of the van's radiator.

"You could've killed us," I yelled. "You had to—you had to reach for the fucking lighter. What the hell are we going to do now?"

"I don't know, Joe, but I'm pretty sure this is the last brew"—he toasted me as if it was New Year's—"so we definitely have to restock." He chugged his beer, still holding his dick in his other hand although he was done pissing.

"Oh, shit." I kicked the van's bumper and hammered my fist on the hood, not to leave any doubt of how mad I was.

I scampered down from the wreck to the Border Highway and tried to figure out where we'd ended up. I was still a little drunk but sobered enough from the accident to know we had to get the hell out of there. La migra was more than likely to swarm all over us. The last thing we needed was to be mistaken for wetback smugglers or drug runners.

The buildings downtown were beacons. I decided I'd find a phone, call my brother to come pick us up and call a wrecker for the van. Not telling Steve my intentions, I just started walking. I figured he'd follow.

Neither of us said anything as we made our way west along the Border Highway. There was hardly any traffic, so there was no chance of us hitching a ride. I took a drag from Steve's last cigarette as a sort of truce. We said nothing.

I'm pretty sure we should've embraced the day's earlier events as a sign. We should've taken our teenage thirsts to the isolated desert, like every Friday night. The acres of sand hills surrounding the Lower Valley always cradle our bonfires like a good hostess.

We walked down the desolate Border Highway for nearly an hour. Before we even reached downtown, I had to convince Steve that it was a totally bogus idea for us to swim across the river when the Santa Fe Bridge was just minutes away. I told him that anyone who might catch us wouldn't be so thrilled with a güero and a pocho—two *drunk* Americans—washing up on their side of the Rio. While you have a fifty-fifty chance of the U.S. Border Patrol being professional, I'm certain, the odds are less with the Mexican police.

AVENIDA JUÁREZ

As I had loyally done for years, I followed Steve to the Atomic Punk, one of several bars on "the Strip." This J-town bar catered to hard rock fans: mostly El Paso high school students and Fort Bliss GI's. Steve immediately made himself the center of attention at the bar and challenged others to drinking matches. I stationed myself by the jukebox, a watch guard, daring anyone to pick songs that would further screw up my Friday night.

I kicked back with a bucket of Coronas on ice and invited Van Halen into my head. My hopes were that Eddie's guitar riffs and brother Alex's drumbeats would settle my nerves. Just like the time Steve and I road-tripped to see them in Cruces.

After many beers and the day's misadventures still too vivid, I finally surrendered the jukebox to some rocker chick who was trying to start a conversation. Something about a guitar player killed when a plane landed on his band's tour bus. She wore a Cheap Trick T-shirt and did a decent air guitar. Good signs despite my suspicion of her white-and-purple mohawk. I lied and told her that I didn't know who she was talking about.

I joined my prized drinker at the bar. A row of yard-long glasses, crystal trophies, was lined up in front of him, an ashtray buried in butts and bottle caps nearby.

"Check this out. I think I got more than enough for a carton of smokes and a whole week of Chico's." Steve flashed a wad of bills. I didn't let him know I was impressed.

Unlike El Paso, closing time in Juárez is usually when people decide to go home. Another thing you can count on is that the later it gets the more the Atomic Punk brews excited energy.

My gut was in knots. Like when Steve would switch off the van's headlights and laugh as we drove by the moonlight of the Chihuahua Desert.

"Hey, man, let's call it a night," I proposed.

He grinned, turned back around, and placed his palms flat on the bar. Who did he think he was? An outlaw gambler, John Wesley Hardin or some shit? Ready for the next hand, he said, "C'mon, Joe, a couple more rounds, and I'll have cab fare for us and Marlene."

I assumed the blonde with dark roots and her tongue in his ear was Marlene.

"Do what you want," I said, as the bartender happily set him up again. A pug-nosed GI who resembled the bar's mascot, a ceramic bulldog behind the bar, claimed the stool next to Steve. The GI had already lost a few rounds. And the hardness of his eyes said he was ready to get even. One way or another.

"My amigo, Ho-say, can be such a tight-ass," Steve told Marlene. She ran her hands through his David Lee Roth mane.

I gave Steve the finger. "Okay, pinche gringo. Later."

He knows better than to call me anything but "Joe."

I was prodded out the door as much by half-sober instincts as by the song playing on the jukebox. I definitely wasn't in the mood, especially this night, to hear Heart whine about dogs and butterflies.

I figured Steve would be there when I got back—either drunk or beat-up and broke, possibly all three—and I wandered out onto the Strip.

Shoeshine boys bragged their expertise.

Tarahumara Indians peddled pottery.

Countless vendors sold food along Avenida Juárez.

The smell of meat and chile and onions cooking on homemade skillets enticed my empty stomach. However, Steve's stories about doggie burritos and kitty tortas spiced with pico de gallo and avocado steered me away. I dropped my ass on the sidewalk. Thinking of the spilled tacos rolling around Steve's van, I scraped hardened Chico's cheese sauce off my high-tops. The sights and smells of the Strip stimulated my senses.

"¡Riiicas! . . . ¡Tooorrrtas! . . . ¡Deliciiiooosas!"

An old man in a never-washed apron called out to passing throngs of wasted teens. The viejito chopped his ingredients and flipped his spatula with the skill of a samurai. He stuffed many tortas for his willing customers.

The flashing neon signs of the Copacabana and Tequila Derby hovered on the other side of the street. This is the world of dance music Steve and I avoid like the Duran Duran styles and Flock of Seagulls haircuts that many of our classmates mimic. I busted up at guys applying eyeliner, using mousse, and wearing anything other than jeans and T-shirts.

I could've sat there till daybreak, witnessing other MTV posers stumble out of the Juárez discos, if a roaring noise hadn't drawn my attention.

Soccer game? Parade? At this hour?

I left the viejito selling his late-night lonches, and I joined the pedestrian line on the Mexican side of the bridge. At the turnstile, a shoeless girl put a hand in my face and begged in Spanish. As much as I understood, she wanted something to eat—not for her but for her dog. A rheumy-eyed mutt licked its balls nearby. I was glad when a Boy George–wanna-be handed her some coins.

SANTA FE BRIDGE

Pursuing the noise, I began the steep walk over the bridge back to the U.S. side. I was tired, and it felt like I was carrying someone on my back. Numbness still chilled my limbs. All the drinking had only made my stomach feel emptier. I gripped the handrail, hoping its firmness would pass through me and give me strength, allowing me safe passage to the other side.

A credit to the torta-selling viejito, my sense of smell was most awake now. The exhaust from the long line of trailer trucks waiting on the bridge was like the smoke-filled Atomic Punk. The moldy stench of the river rivaled the thick cloud over the bridge. I inhaled my surroundings.

The noise that had drawn me off the sidewalk grew louder the closer I got to the top of the bridge. It's here that I always utter a reminder: "I just lost my rights," if I'm going to Juárez, or "I just gained my rights," if I'm coming back to El Paso.

From the bridge's peak—where the U.S. and Mexico flags rested motionless, a safe distance apart from each other—I spotted the ever-present star on the Franklin Mountains. It's supposed to be a symbol of some kind, "El Paso's Sign of Hope," as written on billboards all over town. But it always reminds me of hostages. That was when the tradition of leaving it on every night began.

I thought all this, very aware of the high fences topped with barbed wire surrounding me. I might've contemplated this more if the scene below, the source of all the noise, hadn't distracted me.

I walked down to the U.S. side of the bridge. All ten lanes were blocked off. Traffic was at a standstill. Forty to fifty demonstrators faced the INS checkpoints. A woman with a megaphone made a speech. The crowd shouted its approval. Signs danced above their heads.

2 Cities = 1 People	Justicia Para Todos
N O M O R E F E N C E S	Free Bridge

I'd seen parts of these same slogans in headlines as I dug out the Sports section, the only part of the *Times* I ever read. Although I still didn't know what the demonstration was about, I was drawn to the partylike gathering.

"Not that 'No Grapes' thing again." A couple of tourists also observed from the bridge's walkway. They sported straw sombreros and clutched margarita glasses.

"Here, take this. Sign it." A Chicana wearing a T-shirt that read BORDER RIGHTS COALITION handed me a clipboard.

She didn't appear much older than me, so I reluctantly glanced at the petition. The bold type outlined a proposed barrier—"a steel wall"—along the river to replace the present chainlink fence, the Tortilla Curtain, as it's popularly known. I signed the petition, playing it safe, using Steve's name and address.

The Border Rights Chicana asked if I wanted to carry a sign: WILL YOUR CONSCIENCE BOTHER YOU? Although I liked the way her braided hair pointed to her butt, I shook my head. Her tight jeans asked me to change my mind as I backed away.

My sobering instincts demanded my immediate attention when a fleet of Suburbans drove up to the U.S. side of the border checkpoints. The white vehicles had Border Patrol seals on the doors and what looked like federal license plates. Something bad hid behind the tinted windows.

The officials in suits and ties handling the scene communicated on walkie-talkies and directed security guards in every direction. All eyes on the demonstrators.

I'd had enough.

There are some things, I told myself, that I just don't want to take part in. None of my business anyway. I decided to cross the bridge back to the Mexican side. I'd get Steve, with or without Marlene, and we'd catch a taxi. Time to go home.

Many teens were returning to their cars parked on the American side. Going the wrong way, I went head-on with a drove of partiers and was almost swept up in their drunkenness. I stumbled and hugged the handrail to keep from falling into the border traffic.

The moon that loomed earlier was lost behind rivers of clouds. Whether I looked right or left, El Paso and Juárez appeared the same—dark and dirty and dwarfed by mountains. I didn't know if I was losing or gaining my rights.

I was about to turn my back on the mountain star when I heard what I first thought was thunder. A redhead fell back into my arms. She wore a silky blouse that smelled of tequila and lime. I disappointedly pushed her on her way.

Clouds of smoke sprouted up around the U.S. side of the bridge. The crowd of demonstrators below dropped their signs and covered their mouths. Most of them frantically hurdled the waiting vehicles and sprinted past the checkpoints.

The Border Patrol agents wore black riot gear: helmets, boots, batons, shields. An army ready for action.

I ran back down the bridge and pushed scared teens out of my way. By the time I reached the bottom of the bridge, a group of cornered protestors had torn the posters off their signs and stood poised with wooden stakes.

The woman with the megaphone pleaded with everyone to drop to the ground and lock arms: "Don't fight back! You won't get hurt! Don't fight back!"

A showdown: the demonstrators and the Border Patrol.

No one dared move.

Seconds passed.

Someone lit the fuse.

The scene exploded.

For a moment, I considered running to get Steve. But when I saw an agent running toward the Border Rights Chicana, I didn't hesitate. My left forearm over my head, I charged.

"Goddamnpinchimigra . . ."

Bodies. Punches.

"Fuckingputonazis . . ."

Screams. Sirens.

I had the Chicana right in my sights and thoughts of being a hero when I was grabbed from behind. I hit someone—I hope it was the right someone—before I went down. Withstanding countless blows, I managed to turn over, face the border soldier, and see my reflection in her helmet's shield.

The last thing I remember is her kicking me before I was cuffed and dragged to a Suburban. There was little hope that the Mexican girl from Kmart, or, hell, even John Wayne, would come and set me free.

"EL CORRALÓN"

After hours at the INS detention center, I was let out of an individual cell that smelled worse than the infested Rio. I couldn't even imagine the condition of the other cells, where they corralled hundreds of illegals.

I signed some papers, and when I asked for my watch and ID, a

Border Patrol agent said they'd been misplaced. I know I'll never get them back.

I thought about calling home, where my mom would be finding an empty bed soon, but decided I didn't want to do any explaining.

Across the street, in a gas station's bathroom, I plugged up the sink with paper towels and dunked my head in cold water. I managed to see in a graffiti-covered mirror what had become of my face: cuts on my forehead, a black eye, a red lump above my left cheek, a swollen lip.

Inside the gas station, the attendant sat behind a copy of the *Times*. I glanced at the headlines when I asked if he could give me change for a dollar. I scored a Dr Pepper and a lemon pie from the vending machines.

I walked over to this bus stop, which advertises El Paso's annual festival: FRIJOLE FIESTA—BEST BEANS ON THE BORDER.

I know I'm in a bad way when I can't even laugh at the event's mascot: a cartoon pinto bean dressed in a sombrero and serape and sporting a long mustache and huaraches. "Señor Frijole" usually cracks me up.

I arch my back and stretch my arms, trying to work out some of the soreness. My ribs hurt when I breathe in. The rest of my body stiffened with aches and pains.

I squint at the rising sun as I scarf down my breakfast. I'm not sure how early the buses run. Or, for that matter, which one to take. The only thing I'm sure of is that yesterday's numbness is gone.

> > > *Lucero's Mkt.* < < <

MISSING
María del Valle
58 Years
4'11" About 108 lbs.
Brown eyes   Brown hair
Last Seen Wearing: Blue dress, Gray sweater, Orange hat
Last Seen At: Lucero's Mkt.
Last Seen On: Sunday, September 28
Needs Medication
Call 595-1061. Ask for Delia.

The customers who saw the flier posted in Lucero's Mkt. were not surprised. They read it although they already knew about "La Loquita"—as María del Valle was more commonly known. Among the residents of the Lower Valley, gossip was as common as graffiti.

"Can you believe it?" a woman said to her comadre standing by the canned food section.

"I know, what a price. Seis por un dólar." The comadre stuffed tomato sauce cans in the plastic satchel she'd bought at the Mercado.

"No, not the price, comadre. This mitote about esa vieja loca." She pointed to the flier posted by the register.

"Sí. Pobrecita Delia."

"Thank God she has a daughter that cares. If I would ever go crazy, ni lo mande Dios"—she made the sign of the cross—"my sons, los malcriados, would send me away for sure."

"Nursing home, no, qué nursing home. I told mijo if he ever wants me out of my house, he better hope I'm dead or close to it."

"I'll give them a chanclaso if anyone dares kick me out. I'm not tired. I don't need no rest home."

Between las comadres, they emptied the shelf of tomato sauce and carried their groceries to the counter. Rafael Lucero, the store's owner, held up a copy of the *Diario de Juárez*, pretending not to be eavesdropping on the women.

"Don't worry, Rafael. They'll find La Loquita," one comadre said.

"She's probably hiding," the other woman added.

"Oh, I'm not worried," Rafael lied and kept his attention on ringing up the groceries. "I just hope—" He cut his sentence short and handed the women their change.

The two women left the tiendita, still talking about how awful it must be for Delia, María del Valle's only child. They seemed certain that caring for a crazy old woman must be a great burden.

Rafael glanced at the flier. This photo on the smudged copy

was not the same woman who shopped at his store. No, the woman who, until three days ago, had come in every other week was much older than fifty-eight.

In person, she appeared to be twice that age. Her wrinkled face was pale, as if her heart was too busy pumping blood to her swollen calves and feet. She did have all her hair, as in the photo, but it had been a long time since he'd seen it combed. If it wasn't shoved under a knit cap, it roamed wildly on her head. The biggest difference between the woman he knew and the one pictured on the flier was that she was smiling in the photo. He was saddened to know that María del Valle had once been a good-looking woman with a job, a family—another life altogether.

>>> <<<

On the mornings leading to the day that María del Valle would end up missing, she did nothing different. Sit on the toilet till her bowels complied. Wash the sleep from her face. Rinse away the tastes from the night before with mouthwash. Put on clean underwear if she had any. Slip on one of the housedresses that stunk up her closet. Step into her misshapen chanclas.

And like this daily ritual, she could count on the first thing that she heard every morning being the voice. The one that had taken root in her head some time before.

"Get up."

"All right."

"Levántate. I know you're awake."

"Goddamn it, I'm going."

"Don't drag your feet."

"Como fregas, cabrón."

"I want mine."

That's the way her mornings started. And he always got the last word.

She no longer turned on the radio or buried cotton balls in her ears. It was hopeless to pretend that someone else—a man's voice—wasn't present in her head.

She'd also stopped asking others if they heard his voice. She'd tired of them whispering when they foolishly thought she couldn't hear them. But, really, after time, she didn't care if they called her, among other things, "La Loquita." People kept their distance from crazies. She accepted that.

The arguing between her and the voice had intruded in her home and warded off any visitors. First, friends stopped coming over for dinner. Then her neighbors made excuses for not joining her for coffee. And what hurt the most—when she let herself think about it—who knew the last time Delia and her two boys, Miguel and Gabriel, had visited. Ever since her daughter moved to the other side of the freeway—"I want to teach where kids go to learn, not be vagos"—if anything, she called to say that they wouldn't be able to come as she'd promised. "The boys say, 'Hi and God bless you,'" Delia always said before she hung up.

"Ándale mujer," the voice commanded. "The store opened at eight. You're slowing down, vieja mensa."

"I know time. You don't need to tell me." She put on her hat and sweater, not noticing it was on backward.

"If I don't tell you what to do, you'll do nothing all day."

She didn't respond, since what he said was true. She merely walked down the block to Lucero's Mkt. A few cars were parked along the street. Their owners unseen, inside their homes, behind pulled curtains. She knew not to expect any greetings.

Bells rang when she entered the tiendita. On some days, the radio played behind the counter. The rancheras and cumbias reminded her of when she used to dance till sunrise at the Bronco Ballroom. If even for just a moment, this music replaced the voice in her head.

Out of the corner of her eye, she noticed the man behind the counter. His panza stretched his guayabera and exposed his hairy chest, a feature she'd liked in men. She approached the beverage cooler in the back of the store. In each aisle were the many items that she no longer bought: canned vegetables, soups, bags of rice and pinto beans, crackers, cereal.

"There's plenty of deviled ham and mini weenies at home."

"Shut up. I wasn't thinking of buying anything. Don't get me mad."

Laughter filled her head.

Early on, she and the voice had made a deal. She would buy packs of cigarettes for him and bottles of wine for her.

It had taken several trips to the store to decide which brand of wine she liked best. White Spritz tasted sour, as if it had gone bad. Rose Blossom was too fruity, a liquid dessert. Red Rooster proved to be the best for the headaches the cigarettes gave her. The rooster on the label poised its claws like the one her father took across the Río, where "El Diablo" had won many matches.

Two full coffee cups of Red Rooster and her head floated above her neck. At least it felt that way before she passed out on the sofa.

>>> <<<

Rafael stocked a wide selection of cigarettes. He'd only smoked while in the army and now thought it a dirty thing to do, like reading those magazines he refused to sell of naked women. When he'd bought the store, he debated with his son whether or not to carry cigarettes, especially with the number of kids in the Lower Valley.

"They have enough problems," he'd told his son, the accountant, who said cigarettes, like beer, were a matter of profit. Rafael learned that people bought many cigarettes no matter what warnings they were given.

Although he knew what brand María del Valle smoked, he hoped that she wouldn't need any today. In fact, if he made time to go to church anymore, he might have prayed that she pass through his doors a new woman altogether. Either that, or not come in at all.

"Seven," she said as she pointed to the red packs of Winstons.

From her sweater pockets, she tossed out a wad of food stamps. He took the blue bills, although he risked getting in trouble. Many months had passed since he first accepted the woman's food stamps for wine and cigarettes.

"You need to use them for food," he'd told her before. "It's the government, not me. You understand?"

"My checks haven't come yet. Can you do it this one time?" she'd said.

"I could get in big trouble."

"Just this once."

He liked the way she'd smiled at him and brushed her hands on his. When she said his hands reminded her of a Mexican muralist's, he agreed to accept her food stamps. She even invited him over for dinner. They had a good time—eating, drinking, and listening to records: Cornelio Reyna, Jorge Negrete, Javier Solís. And when she kissed him good night and invited him back, he thought it might be the beginning of something good in his life as an unmarried man.

Weeks passed before she returned to the store, and when he asked if she wanted to go out, maybe margaritas and mariachis at the Kentucky Club, she showed no interest. When she stopped making eye contact and continued paying with food stamps, he admitted to himself that she'd only been nice to get what she needed.

That was so long ago, it seemed. To avoid any hassles, over the time of her visits, he'd worked it out to where he would ring up her purchases as food items and, if necessary, put in cash of his own. "I know it's wrong, but what can I do?" he said to himself.

While she barely uttered a few words anymore—no longer

making excuses or flirting with him—he felt somehow responsible for her habits.

It would be worse, he thought, to stop selling her these things
now that she seems to really need them.

His arrangement with the stubborn woman had recently be-
come more complicated. He'd received a certified letter from the
Texas Department of Human Services addressed to "Mr. Raphael
Luzero, Business Proprietor." The letter informed him that their
office would cease distributing food stamps. A new system, Lone
Star, would be in place this month, he read in the letter, and by
law, he would have to make the necessary changes in his business.
Or face serious fines and penalties.

The letter intimidated Rafael. He didn't have the money to pay
any fines—he'd already borrowed more than he'd ever wanted
to—and he definitely didn't want to end up in jail. The letter
didn't say that, but he concluded that's what would happen. The
State of Texas was big and could, he feared, easily take all he
owned if and when it wanted.

"Tell her the food stamps won't be good anymore. Don't be
such a pendejo," he told himself. "The vieja's gonna get you in
trouble."

The words were wadded tissues in his mouth.

La Loquita stood before him, staring at the cracked tile floor.
Her fingers fidgeted with her ears.

He placed the bottles of Red Rooster and packs of Winstons in
a paper sack.

Go on, tell her, he thought. Make her understand.

No matter what he said, he knew she would be upset. Other
customers had come in the store, and he didn't want to make a
scene. She only half listened anyway, he'd learned when he tried to
ask her out on a second date.

Knowing she'd been a teacher, he slipped a Lone Star pamphlet
in her bag and figured she'd be able to understand it. He

mumbled good-bye and hoped that she'd do what was necessary before her next visit.

>>> <<<

Before she lit a cigarette, she poured herself a second coffee cup of Red Rooster. She was about to throw away the grocery bag when she saw the pamphlet. The Texas flag, like the one outside North Loop Elementary, reminded her of the only job she'd ever had.

She considered that she might have enjoyed teaching such things as state flags, flowers, capitals. Houston? Austin? San Antonio? Definitely not El Paso. She barely remembered her days of teaching, much less any specific lesson. The details of that part of her life were as hazy as the cigarette smoke that smelled up her home.

"What are you waiting for?" the voice said. "You've had yours. Give me mine."

Her first reaction was to tell him to wait, let her think, but it was too early to argue. She resigned herself to lighting a cigarette on the gas burner, raising it to her cracked lips, and sucking hard. Her lungs filled with smoke. He silenced.

She couldn't remember if that man at the store had said anything about the pamphlet. When she unfolded it, there were too many words to read under the heading "Department of Human Services." She tossed the pamphlet in the trash.

She stopped thinking about money soon after North Loop's principal called her into his office one Monday morning. He spoke for a whole class period while she said nothing. A headache from a long weekend pulsed behind her bleary eyes. Her early retirement was the best thing, he assured her.

Soon after, a routine began. Each month, Delia came over, sorted through her mother's mail, paid bills, dropped off her medications, and filled her cabinets and refrigerator with groceries.

Once her daughter went back home, she left all but the canned foods outside for the dogs that roamed the neighborhood. She also had stopped taking her medication a long time ago. As long as the food stamps came in the mail and Lucero's Mkt. had what she needed, the days passed without too much trouble.

She lit another cigarette before the first one burned out. Not wanting to hear the cries of the smoke alarm again, she opened the sliding glass door. Although the grass in the backyard was many shades of yellow, she turned on the sprinkler. Water brushed against the pine trees and rock walls.

The ticking motion of the sprinkler was a sound from her past—a clock one of her ex-lovers had given her as a birthday gift or, maybe, for Valentine's. The face of the clock was a moon, and it had glow-in-the-dark stars at the points of each hour. While whichever man she'd brought back home from the Bronco Ballroom and let into her bed was on top of her, she listened to the clock's mechanical rhythms. Even with Alberto, the one who groaned like an engine on a cold morning, focusing on the clock took her mind far from where her body was.

That's what she hoped for with the sprinkler. As long as she smoked, it was the only sound she heard. She stuffed her sweater pockets with loose cigarettes to guarantee some time alone. This was a relationship she'd resigned herself to, like so many others in her life. *Manny. Vincent. Jesús-Felipe. Eugenio.*

>>> <<<

Rafael considered taking some of his lunch, a pot of caldo de res, over to María del Valle's. By how she'd looked in recent visits, her complexion the color of moldy cheese, he was sure that she'd not eaten a good meal in some time. He stopped asking her why she didn't buy food when she told him it was none of his business. But if you come into my store, it is my business, he wanted to tell her, but he said nothing.

Why do you let her get to you? he thought to himself while

chewing a caldo-soaked corn tortilla. What about the other viejitos? Don Rayo, a blind man. Why not take him some caldo? Apolonio, who's even friendly. He always asks how I'm doing before he begins his own complaints. Why not spend time talking with Doña Enríquez? Pobre mujer. This woman, who he'd heard others gossip about, had eight children, several who were either in jail or doing things that would surely get them there. Despite his loyalty toward his customers, the only one he worried about was María del Valle.

"Forget that vieja enojada," he told himself. "She's nothing but a cold woman who smokes and drinks too much."

He finished eating his lunch listening to Radio Cañón. The rancherita station kept him company while he was alone in the store, especially during the noon hour when business was slow. The busiest times were mornings when people bought the newspaper and pan dulce on their way to work and afternoons when the neighborhood children paraded in after school. They were his favorites. Although he knew that many stole from him and he suspected they were the ones responsible for the graffiti he had to paint over, he didn't close his doors to them.

"It's just candy and gum," he'd told his son when he caught one boy leaving the store with swollen pockets. When his son said they would steal the store from under his eyes, he said he kept the more expensive treats—chicharrones, sodas, ice cream—close to the counter, so when the kids did have money, they'd buy these from him.

Growing up, Rafael had enjoyed a tiendita like his every day after school. The owner, Mr. Mauer, always had a lollipop set aside for him. "Here you go, Little Rafa. Tell your mamacita I said hi," the nice gringo would say. No one had called him "Little Rafa" in many years. All the boys and girls who came into his store called him "El Gordito."

"At least it's not 'Panzón,'" he'd told Doña Felipa one time when she scolded some kids to show respect and call him "Don Lucero."

"That's okay, señora. I am a gordito," he'd told the woman.

He figured she was a little sensitive about her own weight, and he said to the boys after she left, "Don't listen to La Gorda."

The chavalillos left his tiendita laughing and chewing their stolen candy.

>>> <<<

Maybe the worst thing about drinking four coffee cups of Red Rooster before bed was that she often wet herself before she could make it to the toilet. She stripped off her soiled underwear, and as she tossed them in the closet, the stench of urine reminded her of Tavo. She rarely thought about him anymore, but strong odors, like the stink of rotten meat, resurrected him. Whenever her toenails stabbed her as she slept, she also remembered how she put up more with that mugroso than she ever did with any man. At least his pedos didn't smell up the whole bed, like comosellama.

As she sat on the toilet, the hypnotic dripping of the showerhead conjured up the past. She'd found the dachshund outside of her house bleeding and licking its wounds. She never liked dogs—all she'd ever had as a girl were parakeets—but because of how pitiful it looked, she took it in and thought that maybe Delia would let the boys keep it.

The first week she locked Tavo in the shed out back. The dog slept on an old bathrobe. Once it got better, she let it loose in the backyard, where it made a mess: shitting by the porch steps as if it knew exactly where she would walk and digging up the garden she worked on after school. She named the dog Tavo for a mojadito she'd dated. A good dancer and better lover but a hard person to like. They were both small but big pains.

As it turned out, Tavo—the dog, not her lover—was better behaved inside than outside. She first let the dog in one day during a rainstorm. Tavo crawled under her bed, afraid of the thunder, and stayed there, it seemed, until the day it dashed out her door. She'd always thought of the overdressed people who rang her doorbell early Saturday mornings as a bother. And since that day Tavo slipped past her and a man saying something about the light of heaven, she detested visitors, especially those preaching pendejos.

In the dark bathroom, her insides stirring and her butt numb from sitting on the toilet so long, she felt shadows of the emptiness that she'd lived with after Tavo ran off. She searched the Lower Valley, paid some of her students to help her, and, as a last resort, posted fliers, offering a cash reward for Tavo's return.

She kept this up for weeks, finally giving up when the man at the county humane society told her that most dogs Tavo's size didn't stand a chance on the streets. That was when she took to spending her evenings alone on the sofa, sipping wine from a coffee cup, and falling asleep watching telenovelas. *La Luz de la Mañana. Calle de Angeles. Semillas de Amor y Dolor.*

"Vieja, get up." She stood and wiped herself. "Right now. I need mine."

>>> <<<

The hardest thing Rafael felt that he would have to deal with was that his customers, especially the viejitos, kept forgetting their Lone Star numbers. He'd preached to more than one already that they needed to remember it as if it was their Social Security number. "It's that important," he told them. With a hint of guilt, he memorized as many of their personal identification numbers as he could for the next time someone would forget.

He felt good about the new machine that he placed next to the cash register, as the manual instructed. The Lone Star machine wasn't anything like he had feared. The number pad wasn't large and flashy like the scanners they'd recently started using at the convenience stores. His son had taken him to a Good Time Store a few blocks away.

"Miranomas. Not only do they sell cigarettes and beer, but you can get gas también," Rafael, obviously impressed, had told his son.

While everything was beginning to work with those black lines and small numbers on product labels, he still punched in the grocery prices on his register. The scale he weighed produce on was a manual one too.

"I don't need no machine to tell me which things are taxable," he'd told his son proudly when the Good Time Store cashier had trouble with the scanner.

The arrival of Lone Star would change little in the way he did things. No tiene chiste, he thought once he plugged in the right wires. The logo, a star, even reminded him of his grandsons' favorite football team, Los Cowboys. He enjoyed having his grandsons over to watch the games on Sundays. He made them chile con queso and let them take as many bags of tostadas and boxes of animal crackers as they could eat from the store. "Of course I spoil them," he told his son. "What good is a tiendita if you can't open your doors to family and friends?"

The first days of Lone Star had gone by without too much trouble. Only one customer, Ms. Tirres, had forgotten her card and had to return later to pick up her groceries. She complained, but he found that most of his customers liked the "Tarjeta Lone Star."

"Es como una credit card," Don Rayo said. "So, you think they'll take it at La Popular? How about J. C. Penney's?"

"I don't think so," Rafael said, chuckling at the man's enthusiasm.

"It's easy," he explained to Doña Enríquez. "You give me your card. I slide it through here, and you punch in your number."

"How does the machine know how much money I have?" she asked.

"It just does. The stripe keeps track," he assured the woman.

Doña Enríquez looked at the magnetic strip on the back of her Lone Star card quizzically. She wiped her fingerprints off and put it back in her wallet.

He was ultimately glad to know that this change by the state hadn't affected his customers' lives too much. The people in Austin don't always have good ideas, he thought, like that whole cosa called the "blue law."

From the circled date on a Price's Dairy calendar, he knew to expect María del Valle this morning. He was nervous, as if, after all this time, he was taking her on a second date. And like with the one they'd had, he didn't feel good not knowing what would happen. He was so worried that his stomach made noises that escaped out of his butt. Time raced too fast for him. The small hand of the Budweiser clock above the door sounded like rustling leaves.

When he greeted her, trying to sound happy to see her, she merely raised her hand, as if shooing away flies, and hurried past the aisles of food to the cooler. She was getting shorter, it appeared, or was it that he'd moved the Red Rooster to the top shelf?

"She's still a customer," he told himself. "Treat her like everyone else."

Cradling wine bottles, she walked up to Rafael. "Seven," she said and pointed to the stand behind the counter. She tossed the faded food stamps in front of him.

"Oiga, María." He paused. "¿Tiene su tarjeta?"

"What?" she dug a finger deep in her ear, as if she was trying to clean out weeks of wax.

"I need to have your Lone Star card," he repeated. He put his hands on the number pad by the register to show her what he meant. When she didn't respond, he pointed to the sign posted under the register: LONE STAR. SE ACEPTA AQUÍ.

Last night, worrying about her visit, he'd decided that if he couldn't say the necessary words, then he could show her that she couldn't buy wine or cigarettes with food stamps. He wouldn't be the one to give her the news. Lone Star was his way out. It's like having someone from the state in my store, he reasoned to himself. At least that was his plan. And it was his only one.

She tilted her head and stared blankly at him. Her eyes were bloodshot. Snot was crusted around her nostrils. Skin flaked off her scabbed lips.

"I need your card, or money," he said, drawing back the cigarettes and wine.

"I"—there was a long pause—"los cheques"—a longer pause—"no." She ended her words with a weak reach for a bottle.

"You can't." He snatched the items from the counter.

He waited to see what she would do, not sure of what he should do.

"Just give her a pack and a bottle," a voice in his head told him. "Let her go."

But I can't. No, this isn't candy, he thought, coming to understand how neither of them could afford this transaction anymore.

"Mira, if you bring me your information, I can show you how to fill out the forms," he said to her. "It don't take that long."

Her head jerked in response.

"¿María del Valle, entiendes?"

Her body shook. Her fingers corked her ears. Piss ran down her legs and puddled on the floor.

"What's wrong?" he said. "Are you sick?"

His words rang in her head.

"Take my hand."

"Take them. Take them. Go."

"Shut up. Shut up."

"I need mine."

She rushed out the door. Bells rang. She ran down the block. Dogs barked.

"Now what are we going to do, pendeja?"

"I'm going home."

"Go back. Don't listen to that pinche gordo."

"Hombre, vete al demonio."

"Vieja loca, no seas cabrona."

She charged into her house and scoured the kitchen cabinets. There has to be cigarettes here, she thought as she rummaged through drawers. Keys to who knows what, hardened pieces of Juicy Fruit, electrical tape, razor blades, matches, spools of thread, loose Band-Aids, expired coupons, pennies and pesos, green and gold stamps. No cigarettes.

She headed to the bedroom.

"I need mine. Need— Need mine."

On her knees, she ransacked her closet and found only empty, crumpled packs in her sweater pockets. Her dresser drawers were crammed with ungraded papers, full medicine bottles, and un-opened letters.

"Mine, vieja mensa."

"All right, goddamn it."

She went back to the kitchen and checked the sink. Next to a stack of moldy cans of half-eaten deviled ham were stained coffee cups. Bloated cigarette butts that looked like squashed cock-roaches floated in ashy purple water.

"Go back. That stupid gordo has mine."

"I can't."

"Yes, you can. You will. You have what men want."

"Cállate el hocico. You don't know."

"Need . . . Need . . . Need . . . Need . . ."

The voice became a vibration. A ringing. A wailing. A fleet of sirens trapped in her head.

The alarm forced her out of the house.

She ran. Screamed. Covered her ears.

The louder the noise became, the faster she went.

Everything around her a blur.

She tripped in a pothole.

Momentum carried her forward.

Time passed, and the shrill in her head was muffled by exhaustion. After collapsing in the street, she crawled over to the sidewalk, pebbles and glass embedded in her palms.

No one driving or walking by paid attention to La Loquita. The image of Tavo bleeding flashed in her mind. The dog had been smart and whimpered for help.

The sun emerged from behind a cloud. She squinted tears. Reaching the tiendita on her hands and knees, she leaned against the front door. Lucero's was her last hope.

She hoped Rafael would let her in. The radio would be playing. "Turn up the volume," she'd tell him. "Give me your hand, let's dance," he'd say. One arm on her shoulder, one on her waist, he'd lead her up and down the aisles of groceries. Her heart would have a new rhythm as he'd pull her closer to him. Pressed against his hairy chest, she'd feel warmer than she ever had with any man. He'd be that way in bed, she decided, when he'd kiss her.

With the small amount of defiance she had left, she pushed herself off the sidewalk and peered into the store's window. It was dark inside. All she saw was a weak reflection distorted by a handwritten sign: CLOSED—COME BACK.

A pain rang loud inside her. She fell to the ground. Not knowing what else to do, she put her arms over her head, pushed it between her knees, and pressed them hard against her ears. If anyone had noticed, it might've appeared that she was praying.

>>> **Sacred Heart** <<<

>>> <<<

The ceiling is heaven for Ruly. Angels fly in and out of clouds as if playing a game of tag. The smell of lit candles and songs in Spanish make him dizzy. He walks toward the altar, head tilted back, hoping the boyish-faced angels swoop down and carry him to heaven. His grandmother pulls his arm and leads him to a pew. She kneels, crosses herself, and motions him to do the same. He hurriedly kneels and crosses himself and sits down. His first time in this downtown church, he already feels at home. Sacred Heart's ceiling is heaven.

Ruly's grandmother says the Lord's Prayer, which he practices all the time—riding in the back of trucks, buying candy and gum at la tiendita, before he falls asleep—not to forget, saying it fast, the words running into each other.

OurFatherWhoArtInHeavenHallowedBeThyName ...

His hands in a tepee, he bows his head, wanting to ask his grandmother so many questions. Do angels come only to Sacred Heart? Are they here every Sunday? Do little boys get to be angels? As he looks back up at heaven, images Ferris-wheel in his head and pick up speed as the Mass gets under way. More and more questions. Will you become an angel, 'buelita? Does that mean you won't be in your house but in heaven? This heaven at Sacred Heart?

After spending much time with his grandmother in churches—Cristo Rey, San José, Our Lady of Mount Carmel, and now Sacred Heart—Ruly has had to trust a word he is still learning the meaning of. *Faith.* Before he is old enough to attend Father Yermo Elementary with his brother, Frankie, his grandmother has been his private teacher. One of the lessons she's tried to teach him is that as long as he has faith, there isn't a need to ask so many questions. He doesn't yet fully understand *faith* but decides that his grandmother knows as much as the nuns at Father Yermo since she goes to church every day. She talks with God. That's what she said he does when he prays.

He doesn't mind standing and sitting and standing some more and kneeling and crossing himself, he only knows the short one—forehead, ombligo, shoulder, shoulder, beso—but does it twice when his grandmother scribbles many little crosses on herself. Most of the people in Sacred Heart are as old as his grandmother, no children, only some babies in the back who won't stop crying.

Unlike Frankie, he thinks church is fun, and he watches his grandmother to know when to do what. He's beginning to recognize songs, like when the "Mano" song begins—"*Da la mano a tu hermano, da la mano . . .*"—he knows that's when he'll get to shake hands with as many of those people around him as he can before the song ends. ". . . *mano a tu hermano. Da la mano a tu hermano . . .*" He lets others take his hand in theirs, making a face when a viejita pinches his chubby cheek. She smells like flowers in a bottle, his name for perfume ever since he spilled some of his grandmother's.

The men mostly smell like the barbershop across the bridge in Zaragoza, where his grandfather takes him. While Ruly gets a haircut, his grandfather goes next door. "El Barril . . . El Barril . . . El Barril . . ." flashes in the window. He's told Ruly he goes there to read the newspaper, although he leaves his glasses in the truck. No one else in Sacred Heart smells of Jergens Lotion, the one in the little pink-and-white jar his grandmother buys at Lucero's Mkt.

The end of the pew near the center aisle is the best seat. During the Mano song, the altar boys walk down the bumpy carpet, a blue-green river that doesn't keep people apart. The altar boys shake hands with those lucky enough to be sitting on the end of the pew. An altar boy with glasses that keep slipping off his chato nose shakes Ruly's hand and says, "Peace be with you."

Ruly nods and repeats the greeting in his head. He can't help talking to himself and memorizing words that he knows are special. Next time someone shakes his hand, he'll say, "Peace be with you."

Ruly's two quarters jingle like bells when dropped in the basket of offerings. After the Mano song, men go around with baskets balanced on the end of sticks, like those used to break piñatas. A viejita with skin the texture of a wooden crucifix also puts some change in the basket. She smiles at him, exposing her teeth and gums, the color of old pennies. He scoots closer to his grandmother, who must still have all her teeth, or else how would she chew corn on the cob? He'll watch closely when they go to the San Elizario Kermess, where there are almost as many corn vendors as there are booths selling gorditas.

Do angels eat gorditas after church?

Money is collected and taken to the altar. Sacred Heart pulses with music and more songs in Spanish, a language he visits only at church and at La Loma, the neighborhood his grandmother calls home.

The myrrh incense and rose-scented candles of Sacred Heart, along with gorditas, menudo, and tamales, are Sunday smells for Ruly. Women as old as his grandmother, aprons tied around their waists and nets on their heads, work in the cafeteria adjacent to Sacred Heart. Their hands move quickly, clapping masa into patties. Applause. The fat little gorditas sizzle when dropped in a pan of hot oil—more applause—cooking until they're crisp on the outside and not mushy on the inside. A woman behind the counter cuts a grin in one end of a gordita and squeezes it open like the mouth of a sock puppet. The gordita swallows a spoonful of meat and potatoes.

He weaves his way through the cots and blankets scattered around the church cafeteria. He asks a woman sweeping why they have beds here. The woman says that people who don't have a place to sleep use the cafeteria at night. Ruly sees a man slouched by the doorway. He wonders if the beer bottle he clutches makes him sleepy. He thinks that if he didn't have a bed where he could sleep, he would like to sleep here, close to Sacred Heart, near heaven.

A group, all women and some children, wait in line for menudo. Each of them has an olla—shiny pots like silver dollars; black-bottomed ones; broken-handled ones; deep, fat ones; a chipped yellow one like Ruly's father uses to cook frijoles. Ruly doesn't like menudo much—the meat is slimy like mocos. He thinks of the olla-women as other children's grandmothers who keep softened tissue, Juicy Fruit, and a rosary in their pockets.

One of these women in line walks with a cane. A girl, her granddaughter Ruly thinks, carries their olla for menudo. The woman takes careful steps toward the counter. The skinny girl stares back at him, a gordita half in his mouth. He brushes bits of

meat off the lions printed on his sweater vest. The girl's grandmother pays for the menudo, and her cane thumps noisily on the
wooden floor. He wonders if his grandmother will ever need help
walking. If she does, he'll give her his desert walking stick, a dried
yucca branch that he uses to keep from falling when he hunts liz-
ards in La Loma.

He wishes he hadn't put all the change his grandmother gave
him in the church basket. His mouth is on fire. The gordita
women had warned him the salsa was hot, but he said he liked a
lot of it. He's been eating chile with everything even longer than
he's been coming to church. Hurrying past the line of olla-carrying customers, breathing short and fast and sucking his lips, he
begs for a glass of water.

The women in the kitchen laugh and make sympathetic faces.
"Pobrecito, se enchiló. Dale una soda para que se le quite." They
hand him a red Fanta and tell him his grandmother will pay for it
later. The drink cools the sting in his face. It's no longer as red as
the strawberry-colored bottle. He sniffs and wipes his sleeve
across his nose. The last gordita grins back at him, so he pushes
the chile off the top and chews through the patty of meat and potatoes. He eats straight through the middle of the gordita. "That's
where all the meat is," he tells Frankie every time he makes fun of
him.

When he goes back into Sacred Heart, there are only a few others throughout the church. A man without a shoe—his foot ban-
daged, toenails long and dirty—kneels and prays in front of La
Virgen de Guadalupe. His beat-up crutch, held together by black
tape, lies motionless between him and Ruly's grandmother.

Always after Mass, "rezando por todos," she kneels in front of
an altar overrun in candles: rows of small white ones that flicker
like stars; green and orange velas they sell at Lucero's Mkt.; and
one with a white dove, the Holy Spirit. A pink rosary dangles in
his grandmother's hands, nimble fingers caress each bead, lips
mumble in prayer. Ruly knows she's nearly finished with the ro-

sary because her fingers move around the beads to the crucifix.

He walks along the outside aisle of the pews, counting the Stations of the Cross posted on the wall. Numbers are almost as much fun as words, and he knows there are fourteen pictures in all. When he comes to the last one, Jesus in his tomb, he stops.

Was Jesus scared?

How deep is it?

Is it as dark as Dracula's cave?

Farther down the wall, close to the main entrance, there's a picture Ruly has never seen before. The words "Sacred Heart" are engraved in script below a picture of Jesus. A flame burns inside His chest. Rays of light reach in every direction. A crown of thorns pierces His heart. Blood drips off pointy tips.

His grandmother comes up behind him. "I also have a fire in my heart. It's because I love you con todo mi corazón." He's swallowed by her hug and the word "corazón." His child-heart drums against his chest. Corazón. Corazón. Corazón.

"Vámonos, Ruly. We need to hurry." His grandmother kisses his cheek. "Tu 'buelo está esperando."

Trailing his grandmother, he peers at the flaming heart, covers his chest with an open palm, and thinks, I could be like those trains that eat fire. He's seen them in a library book Frankie once brought home. A gordita-smile pops up on his face when he thinks of what kind of train he could be. He choo-choos outside the church like a long red train blowing columns of smoke.

While his grandmother has gone to the Mexican bakery around the corner, from which more Sunday smells escape, he waits in front of Sacred Heart for his grandfather. He steps to the curb when he sees "El Aguacate," his grandfather's sun-beaten green truck. It comes from the direction of a bridge that leads to Juárez. The door opens and he jumps into the truck.

"Hello, 'buelo," Ruly says. "I like this church. Why didn't you come with us?"

Not looking at Ruly, his grandfather answers, "Tengo muchas

cosas que hacer." His tone matches the loud idle of El Aguacate's motor. "No tengo tiempo para gastar en una iglesia."

Ruly figures those many things somehow have to do with what he just saw him slip behind the seat. He suspects it's one of the same bottles that he's found hidden in the cuartito, a wooden toolshed, where his grandfather keeps his plumbing supplies and "mucho tiradero," as his grandmother says. Ruly's distracted when she gets in the truck and hands him a brown paper bag full of pan dulce.

During the drive from downtown to La Loma, Paisano to Alameda to North Loop, neither of his grandparents says anything. The radio is unusually quiet of Radio Cañón's Domingo Rancheritas. Ruly peeks in the paper bag. It's full of ginger pig-shaped cookies. They are his very favorite sweet bread from the city's many panaderías. He lifts a marranito out by the tail and begins eating: ear, snout . . . Why's 'buelo so quiet? . . . ear, leg . . . Is he mad at us because we go to church? . . . leg, tail . . . Will he ever talk to 'buelita again? . . . belly, belly, belly.

At Ruly's parents' house, his grandmother walks him to the door, where her only son welcomes her with a kiss on the cheek. She bends down and hugs Ruly, the bag of marranito cookies crushed between them. The smell of ginger mixed with Jergens is a good one.

"Te quiero mucho, mi corazoncito," she whispers in his ears. "Don't forget me in your prayers."

He never forgets and wonders why she reminds him today.

From the front porch, he yells, "Good-bye 'buelo," but his grandfather doesn't respond. He is slouched in the driver's seat, the brim of his cap pushed down. Ruly's about to yell again when his grandmother says his grandfather must be very tired "de andar haciendo tantas cosas." Ruly's father gives her a sympathetic look, takes him in his arms, and tells him not to worry about saying 'bye to his grandfather.

They watch through the screen door as the grandmother climbs back in the truck and shakes the grandfather, who pushes his cap up, yawns, and stares straight ahead. El Aguacate grumbles down the street and out of sight.

>>> <<<

Ruly continues to sleep in the top bunk bed, although he's fallen out the past few nights chasing angels in his dreams. Cottage cheese, frog warts, he thinks of his ceiling, not heaven, not a church. When his grandmother heard him ask his father to paint his and Frankie's bedroom ceiling blue with white clouds, an angel or two, she explained why he didn't have to—"Heaven is everywhere. Los angeles siempre están contigo."

Ruly was disappointed, but he felt better when she gave him a framed picture that she'd brought with her from México. He put it at the foot of the top bunk bed. "It's a magic picture of Mary and Jesus," he brags to Frankie. A small light bulb inserted at the top of the frame illuminates Mother and Son in gold light. If he tilts his head one way, there is Jesus, to the other side, there is Mary. Left-Jesus, right-Mary, left-Jesus, right-Mary.

Ruly's eyes rock like a boat on water. When Frankie asks him what he's doing, he says that he's trying to see both Jesus and Mary at the same time, as one person.

Frankie climbs into the top bed and pushes Ruly off. His older brother leans to each side, covers one eye, and then the other. Ruly curiously watches.

"No way, tontito," Frankie says. "I don't think you're supposed to see them together."

Ruly continues staring at the picture until he feels like he's stayed on a merry-go-round too many turns. He rubs his eyes, telling himself he should stop looking at Jesus and Mary, but he keeps it up until everything in the room is blurry.

In past games, he's been an Indian, a soldier, even a teacher, though he didn't think that was much fun, so when Frankie asks him to play Confession, he agrees.

"Do you want to be the priest?" Frankie asks, hanging a Spider-Man sheet from the top bunk bed. "We'll call you Padre Ruly, okay?"

While Frankie kneels on one side of the sheet, Ruly sits very still on the other side wearing a turtleneck that itches and a crucifix, which he won at the San Elizario Kermess fishing booth. He kept the plastic crucifix under his pillow where it glowed in the dark for two days. Frankie confesses that he's acted bad in class, gave some of his chilaquiles to their mutt, sometimes forgets to say his prayers, and other things Padre Ruly already knows. The brothers keep few secrets from each other. When Frankie asks Ruly if he thinks these are enough sins to confess for his upcoming Holy Communion, he says maybe he could think of some more. Some he hasn't yet committed but might. Ruly has many ideas.

"How about not cleaning up Negro's caca in the backyard like Dad says. You hate that. I know you still just wet your toothbrush at night. The dentist says up and down, top and bottom, ten times.

"Maybe you and Vincent will break another window at school. You never know . . .

"You could confess first, take a long time. That way Ramiro, David, and the rest of the guys will know how much they have to be forgiven to beat you."

Ruly once walked into a confessional booth at Cristo Rey thinking that was where priests slept. It looked big enough for a bed and a closet of toys. When the priest asked him how long it had been since his last confession, he said nothing. The priest insisted he answer. Ruly hurried out of the church, making sure to put his fingers in the holy water before he exited, as his grandmother had taught him. Later, when he told her what he'd done, she explained that by confessing your sins, you were asking for forgiveness. From then on, Ruly began keeping a "List of Sins" for his first confession.

1. ate too many piggy cookies and got sick
2. kept moms change from buying snow cones
3. spilled milk and said frankie did it
4. ate candy at store and said I didn t
5. went down la loma where priests are buried
6. took keys and unlocked cuartito
7. moved more of abuelos bottles
8. called maria del valle la loquita
9. prayed she wouldnt find me
10. did it again when I promised I wouldnt

Taking out his Big Chief tablet, where he writes down his sins, he tells Frankie he can use some of them if he wants. His brother laughs as he reads over them, hits him on the shoulder for number three, starts to ask him about number seven but doesn't. His older brother thanks him but says he has enough with his.

They go into the kitchen to get what they need for their game of Confession. Frankie says some of the older kids at Father Yermo have told him and his friends that the holy bread he'll receive at Holy Communion tastes like hardened flour tortillas.

From the back of the refrigerator, Frankie picks out tortillas that have fallen out of the plastic bag and hide with the tamales left over from Christmas. Ruly tears the tortillas into the size of silver dollars. The brothers make faces as they chew and try to swallow. Frankie suggests they wash them down with strawberry Kool-Aid, which is dark like holy wine. They also agree the tortillas would taste better with butter, but there isn't any, so they spread on peanut butter.

Frankie says he'll have to try not to let the wafer stick to the top of his mouth or else he might gag. Ruly doesn't think this part of going to Mass is fun. He spits the lump of tortilla in the sink, drinks a palm of water, and is glad he still has a few years before his Holy Communion.

>>> <<<

Though he plays mostly with the Lone Ranger and Tonto, Ruly has started to collect accessories for his G.I. Joe. Kmart has so many things for G.I. Joe: jungle gear, scuba gear, space gear, fireman gear, racing car gear. He is about to choose the fireman helmet and astronaut suit when his attention is drawn to the highest shelf. SALE—G.I. JOE 4X4 OFF-ROAD TRUCK. From what he can see, it's black, with G.I. Joe decals, has fat tires, and comes with a camper shell. When a Kmart man sees him admiring it, he brings it down for Ruly. There is a toolbox, a spare tire, and more supplies in the camper, the Kmart man tells Ruly. His eyes widen with excitement. Even Tonto will fit, he thinks, Scout can ride alongside with the Lone Ranger and Silver. Ruly wishes he was chiquititito, so he could fit in the truck and drive.

While Big 8 Supermarket is the store for milk, bread, eggs, and a bag of green toy soldiers if Ruly has picked up his room, and Lucero's Mkt. is the tiendita for his grandfather's newspaper and his grandmother's Jergens Lotion—they also have good marranitos—Kmart is Ruly's absolute favorite store. He likes it that while his grandmother picks out a dress for Frankie's Holy Communion Mass and his grandfather gets what he needs to fix a toilet, he can walk over to the toy section and pick out the one he wants.

Thrilled with his G.I. Joe truck, he rushes over to his grandmother. The flashing blue light above her makes him dizzy when he stares at it too long. She digs alongside other women through a cart of underwear, hosiery, and purses. These women remind him of the ones at church—gordita-making and olla-carrying señoras. Other 'buelitas, too, he imagines.

"¿No quieres un juguete, mi ángel?" his grandmother asks him, surprised that he's returned empty-handed.

He points to the G.I. Joe truck on the floor and kneels to show her how it works. She tells him to put it in the cart along with her dress, navy with tiny white flowers and ruffles at the neck and wrists.

"You're going to be pretty in that dress, 'buelita." Ruly grins, pleased that they always find what they want at Kmart.

As she brushes his restless hair out of his eyes, his grandfather approaches and drops a crescent, rubber fittings, and a white tube in the cart. Ruly says nothing when his grandfather's things squash his grandmother's dress.

"'buelo, look at my truck. It's like yours but black." Ruly holds it up. His grandfather effortlessly nods his head and turns to his wife. He hands her a fistful of money and walks out to the parking lot.

Ruly wonders what those things are that anger his grandfather. Ruly puts his G.I. Joe truck in the cart, moving the dress on top of everything else. He and his grandmother walk to the store's shoe department.

When a Kmart attendant fits Ruly's foot for his shoe size, he makes faces, laughing from his ombligo. She tells his grandmother that he has chubby feet. He had hoped his grandmother would forget why they specifically came to Kmart. She says he needs dress shoes and a belt to wear for his brother's Holy Communion. They pick out shiny white shoes with laces. The slip-on ones wouldn't squeeze onto his feet.

Above an aisle of work boots—like the ones he prefers wearing to any other shoes—he notices another flashing blue light. It attracts people as if they were bugs. This cart overflows with men's belts and ties that snake onto the floor. He rescues a white belt with pairs of holes all around it. A bow tie is caught on the buckle. Frankie and the other boys will be wearing one, so he asks his grandmother if he can too. "'buelita, do you like it? It goes with my ice-cream-man suit."

She appears surprised when he shows her the brown clip-on speckled with polka dots. "Don't you want one of these? This one also goes with your jacket." She holds up a long knit tie that will match the cream-colored suit that his parents bought him last Easter.

"But I saw a man on TV wearing one like this. He made me laugh. More than Topo Gigo," Ruly says. "Almost as much as El Chapulín Colorado."

"Sí, mi angelito. Todo lo que quieras." His grandmother bends and kisses his cheek. "We better hurry. Ve con 'buelo while I go pay."

He wants to stay in Kmart with her, but he takes the two quarters she offers and puts them in one of the machines outside the store. Feeling good about his prize, a Popeye Pez dispenser, he knocks on the window of El Aguacate. He startles his grandfather, who was falling asleep. When Ruly climbs in the truck, he asks, "'buelo, want a candy?" His grandfather sits up in his seat, rubs his eyes, and looks blankly at Ruly. "Do you want a Popeye candy?" Ruly asks again, pulling back the plastic head with a pipe in its mouth. His grandfather shakes his head. Ruly pretends not to notice when his grandfather takes a drink from the bottle he keeps under the seat.

He wants his grandmother to hurry. More excited about his G.I. Joe truck than his Holy Communion shoes, he imagines pushing it around La Loma's desert, making it go over rocks and sand dunes. He wishes he were old enough to drive. That way his grandfather wouldn't get mad because he has to wait for him and his grandmother all the time.

> > > < < <

The images in Ruly's head are not dreams. A gray light illuminates La Virgen de Guadalupe. Her eyes cast on him and an angel cradles roses at her feet. Where am I? He sits up and rubs his eyes. The light comes from the black-and-white TV. I'm safe, 'buelita's bed, La Loma.

The man on TV with a sombrero and mustache is on horseback, speaking Spanish to a pretty young woman with braided hair. She is as dark-skinned as the statue of La Virgencita on top of the TV.

A second Mexican cowboy playing a guitar rides up on a white stallion with a star-shaped mark on its head. The man talking with the señorita dismounts and takes off his sombrero, puts it over his heart and sings. As much as Ruly understands, he's telling her how beautiful she is—"Como las estrellas en el cielo"—and won't leave without her. Ruly's been on a burro; all he would need to be a Mexican cowboy would be a sombrero and to learn to play the guitar.

The sound of washing pans and dishes comes from the only other room in the house. A light bulb in the middle of the kitchen shines a weak shadow of his grandmother, who goes from the table to the sink carrying stacks of dishes. Moving in small steps, she drags her slippers across the unswept cement floor. When Ruly turns around to watch TV, the cowboy is on his horse again, the señorita rides in back and has her arms tightly around him. Her trenzas bounce on her shoulders as they ride off into a valley.

Ruly hears noises outside an open window. They're coming from the cuartito, where light escapes through the slats of wood. What can 'buelo be working on so late? What if he found the bottles I moved? His grandmother sits massaging her hands in the kitchen. Because she looks tired, he decides he better stay in bed and not bother her. More noises from the cuartito. Why does 'buelo like the cuartito more than being inside? More than church?

Thinking about these things scares him, so he rests his head back on the pillow and falls asleep. He dreams of the angels at Sacred Heart. They're on horseback, wear sombreros, and play guitars instead of harps.

In the morning, Ruly doesn't feel his grandmother next to him in bed and wonders where she might be. At the window, he sees her outside by the street, arms wrapped around her as if she's cold in the sun. He goes outside barefoot in his Spider-Man pajamas.

"Are you waiting for the mailman, 'buelita?" Ruly says and hands her a shawl.

"Go back in the house, mi corazón," she says. "I'll be in to make breakfast en un ratito."

"What are you waiting for?" he asks again.

Pulling the shawl over her shoulders, she says nothing. He looks for himself. The caliche road leading up to La Loma is empty.

Walking back to the house, he stops to remove a thorn from his foot. He notices the cuartito is unlocked, its door hanging from a broken hinge. His grandfather's truck is not parked under the tall cottonwood where it should be. Ruly slowly makes his way to the cuartito, stepping on more thorns, when sounds and voices, like from a bad dream, come rushing forth. "Soy yo, abre la puerta." Knocking, kicking, dogs barking. "Quiero dormir, mujer, dejame entrar." Dogs barking, howling, crying. "Go away ... está el niño, no vas a entrar a mi casa ..." Crying, yelling, roaring of an engine.

Later this morning, Ruly thinks he could play all day in La Loma with his G.I. Joe truck, but he knows he needs to go home and get ready for Frankie's Holy Communion. When his grandmother called his father and began crying, Ruly felt bad and started crying himself.

He remembers when he last saw his grandmother cry, around New Year's. That's when his grandfather was in Juárez for a week. Ruly's father told him his grandfather was working over there, but Frankie asked Ruly if he could keep a secret. That's when his brother said their grandfather was drunk in jail. Ruly didn't see why his grandfather couldn't be working across the bridge, on the other side. He does trabajitos everywhere. Frankie just told him to keep the secret, to not say anything or ask any questions. But he has a need to ask questions. "How am I supposed to know anything if I don't?" he tells Frankie.

If this time is like then, his grandmother will be coming to stay at their house. This makes Ruly feel a little better, and he only hopes that she doesn't sob while she prays. When his father and grandmother come out of her house, she isn't crying anymore, but the sad look on her face ignites a pain inside him. When he hears his father tell her that his grandfather "won't change and was never much of a father," Ruly's heart feels hollow, like a waiting tomb.

>>> <<<

Ruly is happy to be in the church balcony, where the choir sits during Sunday Mass. None of the other kids playing around him seem to notice how high they are. He knows that if he keeps coming to church with his grandmother and does his Holy Communion like Frankie is right now, he'll get to play angel games. Sacred Heart's ceiling is heaven.

Below him, the boys and girls from Frankie's class sit in the front pews of the church. Like all the boys, Frankie wears a white jacket, black pants, and a bow tie, one that clips on like Ruly's. The girls wear lacy white dresses with shiny shoes. Some have flowers in their hair. Leaning over the edge of the balcony, Ruly traces the smoke of burning candles slithering upward. He becomes lightheaded from looking down at his brother and up at heaven. His stomach Tilt-A-Whirls, gurgling bubbles like a shaken soda bottle. He burps and feels that he might throw up his breakfast of huevos con chorizo. The bow tie tightens around his neck and makes it hard for him to breathe. He needs some air, so he goes downstairs and walks out of Sacred Heart, forgetting to cross himself with holy water.

A young man stands across the street from the church selling snow cones. A cart is attached to his bicycle, and music comes from a radio tied to the handlebars. Ruly thinks of the circus: clowns piling out of a miniature car, the smell of cotton candy and elephants, and a man sticking his head in a lion's mouth. Ruly pulls out a yo-yo from one pocket and twenty cents stuck to an unwrapped Tootsie Roll from the other. Will the man trade a snow cone for a yo-yo, two nickels, and a not-so-shiny dime? Half lime, half root beer? Ruly puts the yo-yo, which is Frankie's, not his to trade, back in his pocket, takes a deep breath, and rubs his stomach.

I better go back inside, he tells himself. Frankie said to watch so that I learn what to do during my Holy Communion. As he adjusts his bow tie and loosens his belt, he hears the bicycle cart riding off. He notices a man sitting on the steps of a building across from Sacred Heart. A neon sign hovers over him: DOL RES APA T ENTS VAC NCY. Although the man has his head buried in his palms, a cap covering his face, Ruly knows who he is. On the curb, Ruly spots El Aguacate, his grandfather's truck.

What's he doing there? Should I go tell 'buelita? Dad?

His grandfather stands and walks toward his truck, head still bowed as if it's too heavy to carry. Before he opens the truck's door, he looks in the direction of Sacred Heart. Ruly sees that his grandfather has spotted him on the church steps. Neither grandson nor grandfather moves, says anything, each not knowing what is right.

His grandfather waves, but Ruly doesn't, not sure if he's upset with him. Will he make 'buelita cry again? Is it true that he was never much of a father? Can he change? The hole in his heart deepens with each question.

When his grandfather waves for him to come over, Ruly worriedly decides to go ask him where he was last night. Before he can cross the street, the front doors of Sacred Heart open, and a parade of color spills out of the church, parents and children dressed in their new clothes. Ruly moves out of the way before he is swept up in their celebration.

A man holding a camera, two more hanging around his neck, walks backward down the church steps and takes pictures. The boys and girls who have just made their Holy Communion stop at the top of the stairs. An arched stained-glass window hangs over them—SACRED HEART written below a cross with a heart in its center.

The children coming out of the church smile when the cameraman holds up his hands and counts down from three. Frankie is paired up with Lola, the fattest girl in his class. He isn't smiling, and Ruly wonders if it's because Lola smells like chicharrones or because of his missing front tooth.

When Ruly sees his grandmother in the church's entryway, a smile is reborn on her face, glowing like a polished chalice. He goes over to her and they hug. With her heart beating against his face, she says, "Ay, mi Sagrado Corazón, como quiero mi angelito." Ruly's locked in a tight embrace and turns his head so he can breathe, Jergens Lotion and flowers in a bottle for this holy day.

After his grandmother lets go, he looks around the church for his dad, wanting to tell him who's on the other side of the street. Instead, he notices his grandfather walking up the steps of Sacred Heart. When Ruly turns to his grandmother, she appears very surprised to see her husband here. The grandfather's clothes are dirty and smelly, his eyes bloodshot, and when he takes off his cap, his hair makes him look as if he hasn't slept in days.

Ruly thinks one of them might speak, maybe say something— I'm sorry, I forgive you—but before either of them can say anything, he sees his dad stomping up the church steps. Ruly reads anger on his clenched face. His hands are fists.

Not knowing what will happen, his grandfather standing in the way of his father—padre y hijo—Ruly steps in between the two men.

>>> *I&M Plumbing* <<<

Apolonio had passed the courtyard of the nursing home many times before, but today was the first time he stopped and entered.

In the courtyard's center, there was a cement fountain with a statue of an angel-faced boy. He carried a pitcher from which water once poured. The fountain wasn't working, and judging from the boy's chipped limbs and the condition of the round base—drowned with leaves and dirt—it had been abandoned for some time.

Taking a break from his third daily visit with his wife, the retired plumber studied the figure in the fountain. "Qué lástima," he mumbled and imagined a happier boy if water would only come out of his pitcher.

He went back inside the disinfectant-smelling hallway that led out to the courtyard. He passed storage closets full of sheets and towels and rooms 82 through 86, two hospital beds to each room, and entered the room near the facility's main entrance.

The first thing he heard was Mrs. Mercedes calling for Eva. Esta mujer está loca, he thought. He wasn't being mean. It's just that he knew from personal experience what this so-called rest home could do to one's mind. He wanted to go over to the Mexican woman and tell her that Eva, her only daughter, had left hours ago after feeding her lunch. But he decided he'd better not or he'd risk having to hear many questions for which he didn't have answers.

On the other side of the room, his wife slept, or so it seemed. It was hard to tell, since she hadn't spoken or moved voluntarily for many months now.

He examined a face he better recognized in yellowed photographs and gripped his wife's well-lotioned hands. He began to rub her fingers like the physical therapist had shown him. Pressing knuckles and squeezing joints, he shut his eyes and prayed the rosary, starting where he'd left off before walking into the courtyard.

Dios te salve, María
llena eres de gracia,
el Señor es contigo,
bendita tú eres entre todas las mujeres . . .

When he opened his eyes, it was dark outside the room's only window. Reaching in his pocket, he sorted through loose change and aspirins until he retrieved a watch with a busted band. He realized that evening Mass at Cristo Rey was already under way. If he hurried to San José, he could catch the later Mass, but he decided to pray another rosary at home instead. He'd be up a little after dawn and after feeding the gatitos—some his and others strays from around La Loma—morning Mass would put him back on schedule.

Before he left, he made sure his wife was tucked well under the sheets and blanket he'd brought that first night she was transported to the nursing home from the hospital. Hope it doesn't get too cold, he thought as he put dirty tissues, a Spanish *Reader's Digest,* and an empty mason jar in a Kmart bag.

Trying to make as little noise as possible, he inched his way toward the door. No luck. Mrs. Mercedes opened her glazed eyes and called for Eva once again: "Venga mijita, ayúdame. Ándale, no seas mala." She repeated this several times, while managing to bravely raise one of her puny arms in his direction. "Eva, hija . . . ayúdame." Her voice was a scratchy phonograph.

He knew she'd keep it up if he didn't do something to comfort her. From his shirt pocket, he pulled out his rosary and placed it in the woman's palm. As if she were a baby and the string of beads a pacifier, Mrs. Mercedes's otherwise blank face grew what appeared to be a smile.

He decided that if he wanted his wife to get some sleep tonight her roommate would need to be quiet. He left the rosary that Padre Islas had blessed the day of his wife's stroke. The business-like nursing staff would remove the rosary in the morning during the changing of soiled sheets and giving of sponge baths. They wouldn't care if the lonely woman cried for Eva, or God, for that matter, he thought. Mrs. Mercedes was one body among the hundred-plus at the nursing home, so they would stick something in her mouth if she made too much of a fuss. He never forgot his fear of the morning he'd found Mrs. Mercedes gagged with a sock.

In a way he didn't fully understand, he was glad that his wife couldn't speak. Or else she would also be victimized by nurses who confessed that they worked long hours and were underpaid.

>>> The nursing home's superintendent, Mrs. Hennessey, appeared surprised when he offered to fix the courtyard's fountain.

She said they'd always meant to get it repaired but never had the funds. He told her he would take care of everything. Most of the materials, he already had.

After getting her blessings, he went to his truck. He always carried his plumbing tools behind the seat. "Nunca sabes cuando va haber un trabajito," he'd told his grandson many times. Along with his toolbox, he got a flashlight and dragged out a rooter that he used for clearing out drains. "La Víbora Negra," his grandson named the long metal coil.

In his worn army-green overalls, he crouched over—his shrunken size held together by a life of labor—and put his bare hands into the pipe behind the building. From the way it felt, the fountain's drain hadn't been cleaned in a long while. And if his experience with the plumbing of other, newly built buildings was any sign, he knew that the cheapest materials had been used. He would rely on his twenty-eight years with El Paso county maintenance to finish the task.

He felt good to be working on the fountain. Finally, after what seemed like a lifetime of witnessing his wife's decline, he faced something he could fix. The longer he strained at clearing the pipes, replacing all the corroded fittings, and hauling heavy tubing from the back of his truck, the more absorbed he became in his work.

Padre Islas would ask him at Sunday Mass why he hadn't joined him recently for a cup of coffee, not knowing that one of his most loyal parishioners had taken a vow outside of church.

As a compromise, Apolonio had taken to saying his daily rosary while he worked. The time passed quicker. He found that gripping crescents and pliers, tightening the pipes and fittings, was like handling a rosary. He was most at peace when his hands were working.

After another day under the sun, tired and achy, he went home somewhat satisfied. He didn't look in on his wife before he left the nursing home. While his thoughts were of her on his drive home, completing the work on the fountain was his immediate priority. First thing in the morning, he would drive to I&M Plumbing for some needed materials. The store was out of the way, but he thought that he would enjoy the smell of alfalfa on North Loop Road. And he looked forward to seeing an old friend even more.

Manuel, his partner from his days with county maintenance, always had the right supplies for any trabajitos he took on. Having contact with someone who didn't feel sorry for him, he decided, would also do him good.

Before he went to sleep that night, unlike other nights, he didn't ask God why He hadn't just taken his wife that Sunday afternoon rather than prolonging her ascent. After praying on his knees before his dresser—lit velas rested next to a faded print of La Virgen—he fell asleep and dreamt that the boy from the fountain came to La Loma.

The laborer welcomed the visitor into his adobe home. He drank when the boy offered him water from his clay jarra. The boy then went over and gave water to a woman in a hospital bed. Apolonio first thought she was his wife, but when he hurried over to her, he realized it was Mrs. Mercedes. She stood after drinking the water and walked off with the boy.

Apolonio was content on sleeping that night—not feeling too alone—and for quite some time after, he awoke without being thirsty for answers.

> > > The next day, a full coffee cup warming his hand, he listened to Manuel speak of a trabajito he'd done for his compadre's son. The way his old friend explained it, the kitchen sink would continue to leak no matter what he did.

"I'm a good plumber, tú sabes eso," Manuel said, "but when they don't pay me, pos, I replace the washer y me voy."

Apolonio smiled and sipped his coffee, which Manuel had served him although he'd said no thanks.

"Next time he calls, I'll just say my arthritis is acting up."
Apolonio shared in Manuel's laughter.

Every few minutes a customer would come to the counter and
pay for some materials. If they didn't know what it was they
needed or where to find it, Manuel would help them. But only after making a fuss about having to put down the pan de huevo he
was enjoying with a cup of coffee, his third since Apolonio's arrival.

I&M Plumbing on Alameda Avenue was one of the few places
left in the border city that had everything you needed for a
plumbing job. Yes, other stores had recently opened nearby and
were bigger and more modern, and maybe even cheaper, but
these flashier stores made you wait up to a week for some things
you needed right away. Like the model of water heater a man was
describing to Manuel.

"I don't have it here, but come back tomorrow y te lo tengo
listo." Manuel winked as if to assure the man he'd come to the
right place.

"Really, is there an extra charge for that?" the customer asked.

"Qué extra charge?" Manuel pursed his lips. "Oiga, joven, just
come back." He wrote down the man's name and the water
heater's model number.

"Thank you. My family's been taking cold showers for two
days."

"And if you need a good plumber to put it in, this is your man."
Manuel patted Apolonio on the shoulder. "He's the best I know.
Next to me."

The three men grinned.

The customer said thanks but that he would try to install the
water heater himself. Apolonio was embarrassed by his friend's
flattery but silently agreed that he was one of the two best plumbers he knew.

Manuel took out a notepad and phoned the person who could

get the water heater he needed. Apolonio didn't keep a notepad with names and phone numbers anymore, but he, too, knew from who and where in El Paso-Juárez he could get what he needed for any trabajito. That was why he was here today visiting Manuel. Well, at least, that's what he'd told his friend, who he hadn't seen since around the time of his wife's stroke.

"¿Miraste los Dodgers?" Apolonio asked Manuel after he got off the phone.

"No. When they play?"

"El otro día."

"¿Quién les jugaron?"

"Los Padres, no, los Giants. Dodgers won, seis a dos."

Silence filled the next moments. Apolonio liked that they didn't have to talk all the time. This silence—unlike the one with his wife—was comforting.

"Polo, ven, te quiero 'señar algo." The two men walked out from behind the front counter to the sales area. In front of rows of bins filled with pipe fittings of various sizes, PVC and brass, was a display: KING SPEED ROOTER—"GETS THE JOB DONE FAST."

Apolonio pulled on the metal coil and stroked the chrome casing of the electric rooter. If he'd had one of these, he thought, he could've finished unclogging the fountain's drain in no time. The manual rooter he used did the job, but he had to take frequent breaks because his arms, especially around his shoulders, tired from cranking it. Ever since he started fixing the fountain, he had to rub Ben-Gay on himself before he went to bed.

"'sta suave. But too much money." Apolonio stood back and admired the King Speed Rooter, certain it was a better machine than the ones hooked up to his wife.

"The salesman who brought it in told me to put it here, right as you walk in the store," Manuel said. "If it doesn't sell by the end of the month, he said he'd take it back. He gave me some free washers, fittings, and this calendar."

He took the calendar off the near wall and showed it to Apolonio. A redhead in only overalls was posed among assorted colors of sinks, bathtubs, and commodes. Apolonio put his hand under his cap and scratched his balding head. When they'd worked together at the County Coliseum, Manuel had decorated the tool room with pictures from magazines he thought the other workers would like—women in bikinis, new pickups, Carlos Palomino, Fernando Valenzuela.

"Casados" was what the supervisor used to call them. In their marriage, Apolonio was the worker and Manuel the thinker.

Apolonio had always been thankful that Manuel had taught him patience. When they'd met, right after Apolonio came out of the army, his approach to every job was finish it as fast as he could. He felt proud when he did twice as much as other plumbers and his superiors, like Lieutenant Jarvis at Fort Bliss, praised him for it.

"It's no good if you do it fast and you have to go back and do it again in a few months," Manuel had told Apolonio on their first job together, installing the urinals at Western Playland Amusement Park. He learned to listen, take his time, and eventually it worked out to where they would always be partners. Twenty-five years, second only to his forty-three-year marriage.

Behind the counter, they finished their coffees and watched customers enter the store. They would comment on all the purchases, and they agreed that nothing was as good as it used to be.

"When are we going?" Manuel made a drinking motion with his hand, a big grin on his face.

"Cuando quieras." Apolonio didn't like lying to his oldest friend. He knew that he couldn't go drinking like they used to every payday, and he didn't know how to say this without sounding like less than the man he once was. Anyway, his friend wasn't supposed to drink anymore. After his operation a few years ago, the doctors told him to stop drinking and smoking. From the full ashtray near the coffee machine, Apolonio guessed that Manuel had said to hell with the doctors' instructions.

"I could use a cervezita right now." Manuel took a long swallow from his "Viva Las Vegas" mug. Apolonio wondered what his friend kept cool inside the refrigerator in the back room.

They talked about their children. Manuel had always been jealous of Apolonio because he had only one, a son. In Manuel's own words, he'd been cursed with bad luck—four daughters. One was a dancer at the Tropicana, another was married to un Americano and lived on the other side of the freeway, and the other two attended the local college. After Apolonio told his friend that he didn't see his son much anymore, his friend joked that he wished his two youngest would go on and get married and leave him alone.

"I know when they want something. They call me 'Papi' and put their arms around me and tickle my stomach." Manuel went into an adjacent bathroom, left the door open, and kept talking. "They don't like sharing a car, but that's all I can get them. I told them one could drive my truck. 'Yonque' they call it. ¿Lo crees?"

Apolonio found it almost unbelievable that Manuel could still be driving the truck he'd had since before they started working together. It *was* a piece of junk, and he'd told him many times before.

"Comprate otra."

"¿Polo, 'stas loco? Esa troquita es mi sweetheart—together forever."

Manuel walked out of the bathroom and over to a window. The body of the Chevy truck was more rust than blue paint, the hubcaps had been stolen, and cardboard was taped over a broken window. The only thing that had kept it from completely falling apart all these years, Apolonio thought, was the rosary hanging from the rearview mirror.

Shaking his head, he remembered Manuel was as dedicated to Iliana, his wife. After she died about fifteen years ago, work was the only thing that Manuel seemed to care about. Often, Apolonio would get home late because his partner wanted to answer another call, or after clocking out early, he convinced him to go to Zaragoza, across the bridge, for a few beers. Apolonio never had to explain his lateness to his wife. She'd said his best friend needed his company now more than ever.

Apolonio told Manuel that he had to go. The drive to the nursing home was a long one, and he wanted to see if the hose and valves were right for the fountain. Manuel assured him that they were, but if not, he'd be here tomorrow—"Como siempre."

The soon-to-be widower took comfort in this. And he didn't feel as guilty that he'd skipped his morning visit to the nursing home. I&M Plumbing would remain the one place that always had what he needed.

››› A few days passed before news of the working fountain made its way to every room of the nursing home. No longer were the residents satisfied with being placed in front of a talk-and-game-show-happy TV set in the facility's lobby. Even ones that couldn't—or wouldn't—speak somehow managed to communicate to the nurses that they'd rather be outside in the courtyard. Mrs. Mercedes, for one, had Eva wheel her out every morning and evening to see the fountain, or else the mother refused to eat.

The courtyard's centerpiece was not the only object that had been resurrected. Encouraged by Apolonio's success, Mrs. Hennessey had put some staff people to work on the landscape: Flowers from the nursing home's front lawn were transplanted, plump bushes were trimmed into matching shapes, and, in a few weeks, the grass would be alive again with color.

Inside the faded blue walls of room 89, Apolonio only hoped that his wife could imagine the courtyard from his simple descriptions in Spanish. But many doctors were positive that she couldn't hear or see anything, and if she did, she most likely didn't understand it. The stroke, along with her already weak heart and chronic diabetes, had completely wrecked most of her brain. When Apolonio tried to speak with her or get her to move a hand or a foot, he considered a blink a cruel settlement.

To make it easier for Apolonio to understand, a member of the hospital staff had tried to explain his wife's condition in terms he might recognize. The male nurse told him in Spanish that his wife had suffered a stroke, which is like when a machine short-circuits.

Staring at his wife's lifeless face, he remembered thinking that if the stroke she'd suffered was like a machine breaking down, then there must be someone who could provide repair. Doctors are like electricians and mechanics and plumbers, he thought. They can fix whatever's broken. The following months changed how his own mind understood and registered things. His wife's physical state was more than a trabajito.

He placed a new box of tissues and a mason jar on the table next to her bed. Twisting off the cap, he put his fingers in the holy water and made the sign of the cross on his wife's forehead, then did the same for himself.

Intending to pray a rosary before he visited the courtyard, he searched his pockets, then remembered that he had never gotten his rosary back from Mrs. Mercedes. All he had in his pockets were some fittings that he'd replaced on the fountain. Rather than throw them out, he was taking them home, where he had buckets of brass and copper materials among an altar of sinks and commodes in his cuartito.

Sitting on a corner of his wife's bed, he shut his eyes and began a rosary. While the string of recited words comforted him, he winced as he prayed. The sharp edges of the metal fittings stung and creased his fingertips.

Richard Yañez, associate professor of English at El Paso Community College, was born and raised on the US-Mexico border. He is also the author of the novel, *Cross Over Water,* published by the University of Nevada Press.